Courtship at Rosings

COURTSHIP AT ROSINGS

A Pride and Prejudice Novella

Rose Fairbanks

Courtship at Rosings

Published by Rose Fairbanks

©2019 Rose Fairbanks

All Rights Reserved. No part of this book may be reproduced in any form, except in the case of brief quotations embodied in critical articles or reviews, without permission in writing from its publisher and author.

Several passages in this novel are paraphrased from the works of Jane Austen.

This is a work of fiction. Any resemblance to characters, whether living or dead, is not the intention of this author.

Contents

Also by Rose Fairbanks

Jane Austen Re-Imaginings Series

(STAND ALONE SERIES)

Letters from the Heart
Undone Business
No Cause to Repine
Love Lasts Longest
Mr. Darcy's Kindness
Mr. Darcy's Compassion

When Love Blooms Series

Sufficient Encouragement
Renewed Hope
Extraordinary Devotion

Loving Elizabeth Series

Pledged
Reunited
Treasured
Loving Elizabeth Collection (Books 1-3)

Pride and Prejudice and Bluestockings

Mr. Darcy's Bluestocking Bride

Lady Darcy's Bluestocking Club (Coming 2020)

Impertinent Daughters Series

The Gentleman's Impertinent Daughter
Mr. Darcy's Impertinent Daughter (Coming 2020)

Desire and Obligation Series

A Sense of Obligation
Domestic Felicity (Coming 2020)

Christmas with Jane

Once Upon a December
Mr. Darcy's Miracle at Longbourn
How Darcy Saved Christmas

Men of Austen

The Secrets of Pemberley
The Secrets of Donwell Abbey (*Emma* Variation,
Coming 2020)

Regency Romance

Flowers of Scotland (Marriage Maker Series)

The Maid of Inverness

Paranormal Regency Fairy Tale

Cinderella's Phantom Prince and Beauty's Mirror (with Jenni James)

Chapter One

Fitzwilliam Darcy put down his half-empty glass of brandy and paced across his overly decorated chamber at Rosings Park. Finally, he ceased and stared out the window in the direction of the small parsonage in the distance. His cousin Richard chuckled. He had witnessed Darcy's indecision several times in the last fortnight. It was not lost on Darcy that he typically was self-assured and in control of himself. Darcy often paced and stared out windows when making crucial decisions in his role as Master of Pemberley, but this was the first time he had ever acted this way over a woman.

He had left Elizabeth Bennet behind once before. He had told himself in November that his admiration would soon cease. Indeed, when he first arrived in Kent and discovered Elizabeth was a guest at the parsonage, he attempted to stay away. He managed a whole week before he was drawn to her like a moth to a flame. He loved her, but was marriage the best route? Might he sufficiently forget about her with the passage of time and the addition of distance? Darcy's heart squeezed at the thought.

Richard interrupted Darcy's hard-fought-for solitude. "Well, are we leaving as scheduled or not?"

His query was met with silence. Richard tried again. "I take it that means no. I suppose I have another letter to write begging leave again."

Darcy spun around. He met Richard's eyes and answered with determination. "No. We leave on Saturday."

He walked swiftly back to his glass of brandy and swallowed the remainder quickly, allowing the slow burn down his throat to serve as a seal to the resolution in his heart. As he placed it back down, the glass rang out like a bell, lending drama to his declaration.

"Tally ho! I wish you joy, then!" Richard exclaimed.

"Not yet, Richard, not yet."

"Surely you do not doubt her answer. You are the Master of Pemberley!" Richard came to Darcy's side. "I love you as a brother, indeed more than my actual brother. I am not blind to your faults but admire your clear vision of duty and responsibility. You do not lean towards loose living like Ashbourne. With your wealth and station, I doubt any woman would ever refuse you."

"I love you as a brother as well, and your good opinion is invaluable. However, I am unsure my money or standing in society means much to Elizabeth...Miss Elizabeth. She has never sought to flatter me and has always treated me as an equal. Despite this, I must know her feelings, and I can no longer bear the uncertainty and constant restlessness. I have tried for months to forget her. Indeed, given my position and duty in life, I ought not to make her an offer, but she has bewitched me. I know now my life is only an empty shell without her love and laughter."

"Have you thought about what you will say?"

Darcy shook his head. "A man hardly knows and obviously only hopes to do so once. Father did try to teach me, and my mother cherished the memory of the beautiful words he spoke to her during his proposal. I will speak truthfully of my ardent love."

"How truthfully do you intend to speak?" Richard frowned. "I know it's been difficult to reach a decision because of her situation in life and her family's impropriety. Is that not why you separated Bingley from her sister?"

"Yes, but it is a degradation I will happily go through to have her by my side. I see it as another example of my enduring love compared with Bingley's mere infatuation."

"How do you know that all these months later he is not still pining for his Miss Bennet the way you are pining for yours? You also left Hertfordshire behind."

"This is true enough. Although another concern was Miss Bennet's attachment to him. Perhaps Elizabeth can shed some light on her sister's feelings."

"Surely you don't think you should approach her with the subject."

"Why not? There is no shame in my actions and advice towards my friend. I believe even Miss Elizabeth is sensible to her family's impropriety. You should see the mortification they cause her. I will soon relieve her of that pain. At any rate, you know I abhor anything that looks like deceit. She should know of my involvement."

"Yes, but if Miss Bennet did truly love Bingley, you could hardly expect Elizabeth to look favourably upon the man who separated her sister from the gentleman she loved. That information should not come from the man himself during a proposal of marriage! No matter how sensible she is to her family's impropriety, lack of connections, and the degradation marriage to her would bring you, she should not be told outright of it all. She is intelligent enough to know this and will offer gratitude for your addresses. A gentleman should not beat it into the woman he loves."

Darcy reflected on this for several minutes. Although he desired absolute truthfulness between them, he realised his words could only bring Elizabeth pain. Darcy replied, "I never would have thought about it that way. I can see how I would have only made an awful mess of this if it were not for your insight." After another pause, he nervously added, "Now that you mention it, I do fear she may resent my actions towards Bingley. We have not been able to discuss the matter, though she has tried."

"Discuss the matter, indeed! All you do is stare at her!"

"Has it been that bad? Well, you know how difficult it is for me to converse anyway, especially when I fear my tongue will get away from me from months of suppressing my love." Another moment passed, and insecurity crept in once more. "Maybe I do need more time—"

Richard interrupted his words. "Darcy! Do not talk yourself out of this again! If you would like, I can help bridge these discussions and gauge her reaction for you."

Taking a moment to think of the possible outcomes, Darcy replied at last, "Perhaps that would be best. I certainly trust you to phrase things better than I could."

"That is putting it mildly, my cousin!"

Darcy feigned shock and annoyance at his remark. "And when do you propose to act out this little skit?"

Richard thought for a moment. "I could do it during her morning walk tomorrow. After, you can call on her. Mrs. Collins makes her calls in the village tomorrow, and Miss Lucas is always happy to go whilst Miss Elizabeth prefers to stay behind. Just do not be too scared to follow through this time!"

Darcy paced around again before stopping in front of the window and wondered which room Elizabeth was in. The woman had entirely bewitched his heart and soul. All his hopes and wishes for happiness dwelt with her acceptance of his hand. Letting out a sigh that was the only sign of his anxiety and fear, Darcy asked, "Richard, do you think she will accept?"

"Indeed, I hope so only for my sake. Then I would no longer see you hopelessly mooning after her! Put us out of your misery!" The words obviously did not relieve his cousin as he had hoped, and he added, "Goodness, you are far gone, man! You are Fitzwilliam Darcy, Master of Pemberley, over whom all the ladies of the ton fawn. A gentleman, intelligent, generous, and a loyal friend and brother—of course, she will say yes! She would be the biggest fool ever to refuse you. I am certain that it is not possible."

Only mildly reassured, Darcy countered, "But what of her regard? It would be bitter for her to marry me only for my fortune, status, and reputation as a gentleman. I desire her love."

"Do you not see how she teases and plays with you?" Fitzwilliam asked incredulously.

"She does, yes. But is that regard? She smiles more with you. I have even seen her enjoy George Wickham's company!"

"It is true she is a pleasant conversationalist, but her treatment of you is different. She clearly enjoys your heated debates, and whilst Wickham has charming manners, I am sure she can see his shallowness by now, even if she does not know of his evil deeds. I thought you told me that he scampered quickly after some young thing who inherited ten thousand pounds. Surely she could see through that."

"Sometimes I worry she aims to wound," Darcy spoke softly, afraid to voice his most profound worry.

"I have not seen evidence of that. Why would she take a dislike of you?"

"I was not well-liked in Hertfordshire. You know my reserve comes off as pride, and I did find the country company less than desirable. At the Meryton Assembly, I was nauseated by the fortune hunters. I know I immediately gave a bad impression. Bingley begged me to dance. To put him off, I said Miss Elizabeth was merely tolerable and not handsome enough to tempt me without even looking at her first. It was quickly repeated throughout the assembly. I saw no sign that it affected Elizabeth, though, and I have tried since to show that I was wrong and am not disgustingly proud."

Darcy shook his head and grit his teeth. Recalling the tension of the Netherfield Ball, he spewed out, "Who knows what Wickham has been saying? I know he has sought to wound her opinion of me." Why was Wickham once again ruining his chance of happiness?

"Surely she is not so prejudiced! Besides, she has interacted with you very frequently now, whereas most of Meryton has not. I have never known you to care for anyone's opinion of you, let alone country society."

"I do value the opinions of those I esteem and respect. I value and covet Elizabeth's good opinion."

"Well, I believe you have it and that your worry is for naught. Tomorrow we will find out!"

Gazing out the window one last time, Darcy turned back to his cousin and responded a bit more hopefully than before, "Yes we shall! And with any luck, I will ride for Longbourn early next week!"

"That is the spirit! Come, we must re-join Aunt Catherine and the ladies now." Fitzwilliam walked over to where Darcy stood, obviously still half in his own thoughts, and clapped him on the shoulder, almost making him jump.

Chapter Two

Gathering up her gloves and bonnet, Elizabeth Bennet bid her friends Charlotte and Maria farewell. "I suspect you will be off before I return. I have had a new letter from Jane, which I will enjoy reading whilst I am out."

"I do hope you enjoy your walk, whether it is in solitude or with a companion." Charlotte smiled and raised her brows.

Elizabeth rolled her eyes at the allusion to Mr. Darcy, who had interrupted several of her latest walks.

"Charlotte, please. We have talked about this. Now, I'm off!" Elizabeth tried to express more certainty than she felt.

Mr. Darcy confused her. Even in Hertfordshire, she often found him staring at her. He conversed more openly with her there, such as during her time at Netherfield. Here he rarely spoke, especially in any coherent fashion. If she were honest with herself, she began to think it was not out of criticism as she had initially thought. However, she could not entertain the thought that he might regard her affectionately.

"Perhaps not, and yet I would not wish to marry a lady solely for the weight of her purse. Generally speaking, a man would wish to give his bride a better home than her father. There is no matching Darcy there."

Elizabeth scoffed. "What ridiculousness! Are there truly men who go around refusing to offer marriage to ladies if their income does not match their beloved's father?"

"Despite the appearance of my sex, there are expectations of us, and this is one of them. It would be quite intimidating to propose marriage to a rich lady and have little independence."

"And yet that is precisely what you have explained to me is expected of you."

"Now you know why so many younger sons do not marry at all."

"Do you not see that by refusing to have the courage to offer their hand in marriage to a lady whose father intimidates them, these men condemn ladies to spinsterhood? There are already far more marriageable ladies than men in the country at present."

"You may be correct. All I can say is that it would take great assurance on the part of the lady to make it worth the man's while."

Elizabeth wondered if his statements were meant for her. She had liked him but did not desire his proposal. How could she put an end to his curiosity?

"Alas, it makes little difference to me. I am too poor to be the centre of attention for a suitor without independent means."

Colonel Fitzwilliam did not immediately reply and looked at her with a pensive expression. Hoping to avoid further talk of his own marital prospects, she inquired after his cousin.

"You say you are at Mr. Darcy's disposal. Was that his ambition in bringing you with him? Perhaps he should marry to have a lasting convenience. However, I hear he has a sister, and she might do at present since she is under his sole care."

"Alas, for her sake, I share the role of guardian to Miss Darcy."

"Indeed! What kind of guardian do you make? Does she give you much trouble?"

Colonel Fitzwilliam stopped walking and looked at Elizabeth with such an alarmed expression that she immediately reassured him. "Do not fear. I have not heard any ill behaviour on her part, and due to her status, gossip would surely abound if there was any to be had. I only know what I have heard of her from Mrs. Hurst and Miss Bingley. I think I have heard you mention that you know them."

The colonel visibly relaxed. "I know their brother far better. He is excessively pleasant and a very great friend of Darcy's."

"I am sure some would say he takes excellent care of Mr. Bingley." Elizabeth's mouth twisted with bitterness.

"What a way with words you have!" Colonel Fitzwilliam chuckled. "I suppose in his own way, yes, Darcy does take care of Mr. Bingley. I believe Darcy lately saved his friend from an imprudent marriage. Although I do not know for certain that it was Bingley.

I only think so because they spent the whole of the summer together."

It was now Elizabeth's turn to nearly miss a step. She recovered quickly and affected an impassive face. "How curious. What reasons did Mr. Darcy have for separating the two?"

"There were strong objections against the lady."

Objections against her Jane? Impossible! Jane was the sweetest soul who ever existed.

"Perhaps I may ask Mr. Darcy what arts he used to interfere. As a lady, I have had more than one friend marry where I would not recommend." She said it saucily but realised there was a ring of truth to it. She had attempted to change Charlotte's mind about marrying Mr. Collins, and more than once she had pointed out a deficiency in a suitor of Jane's.

"I confess I expected you to dislike my tale more."

"Why is that? I do not agree that Mr. Darcy had any right to tell his friend where to marry. However, I will concede that I do not know all the particulars and must assume there was not much affection in the situation." Elizabeth breathed a sigh of relief. She had effectively made the colonel believe she was completely unaffected by this news.

"Perhaps so. It does lessen my cousin's triumph, but as the gentleman had a large fortune, I cannot conceive of another reason he would not marry where he wished."

Elizabeth allowed the subject to drop, and they spoke of the surrounding countryside until they reached the parsonage.

After he departed, Elizabeth went straight to her room and reviewed the information she had learned. She had suspected Miss Bingley held the greater share of the blame for separating Jane from Bingley. To learn it was Mr. Darcy, who all this while in Kent acted as though he had not ruined her sister's happiness, was a blow indeed! Colonel Fitzwilliam had spoken in jest about Darcy's triumph, but it fit perfectly with her understanding of that man's character. The proud man would rejoice in what he had done. She never wanted to see him again.

Tears began to flow as she realised she had been a fool to look past her first impressions of Darcy. They were always right. The Mr. Darcy she thought she was beginning to know never existed at all—he was all pride and conceit. She should have recalled Mr. Wickham's story of misuse. He had grown up with Darcy and was abused by him. What more could Elizabeth hope for Jane? Whilst only a few hours ago she had considered it possible for Jane to learn to love another, it was no consolation upon learning that Jane was torn from Bingley by the whims of a man with intense pride.

By the time the clock struck the hour to dress for tea at Rosings, Elizabeth's head pounded so hard she could barely form words. Charlotte could see how ill Elizabeth was and quickly excused her friend, leaving Elizabeth in miserable solitude. Why had it pained her so much to have confirmed what she had, until recently, suspected? Elizabeth did not dare to fathom an answer to the question.

Chapter Three

Listening against his door, Darcy heard the unmistakable sound of Richard's boots as he walked down the hall. As Richard neared the door, Darcy opened it and pulled his cousin in. "Did you see Elizabeth? What did you say? What did she say?"

Richard laughed. "Eager, are we?" He settled into a chair and waited for Darcy to do the same. "Yes, I did see her. I opened by talking about the disadvantages of being a younger son, not being able to marry as I wished due to lack of fortune and connections. She took no insult and seems to understand entirely what her position is. She observed, correctly, that you prefer to have your own way much of the time and slyly suggested that you take a wife to have someone at your disposal to order around."

Darcy frowned; this did not seem like the type of treatment Elizabeth would desire in a marriage. As it was not how he intended to behave, he sincerely hoped she did not expect him to think in such a way.

Richard continued, "She asked if Georgiana was spirited and caused us trouble. At first, I worried

Wickham had told her something, but she swore she has heard no evil of Georgie. I think Miss Elizabeth wanted to know how you would handle a high-spirited woman in your life. I had hoped to mention your loyalty as a brother, but she brought up Bingley. I said you were such a great friend to him and gave a little story of how you separated him from an imprudent match. However, I was clear that I did not know names and other, just that you counselled him against it. She seemed quite agitated about the matter but, in the end, commented that there must not have been much affection on his behalf. I am sure she understands why you interfered and that only the deepest love could make a man overlook all these matters. We then talked of other things and parted quite happily. She must love you to want to know these things about you."

Upon hearing Richard's statement of the facts, Darcy saw that it was entirely arrogant of him to interfere with Bingley. Jane Bennet was no fortune hunter. Darcy was merely prejudiced from his experiences on the matter. Additionally, he could not complain that Miss Bennet did not display emotions openly whilst simultaneously complaining that the younger Bennet daughters and their mother showed too much. Darcy considered how it might feel to be abandoned by the one you love without any explanation.

He pondered how he would feel if someone did that to his own beloved sister. How badly had he injured Elizabeth over this? Had this caused her much pain? Had it made her cry? The image of a crying Elizabeth made him hate himself.

Richard interrupted Darcy's dark thoughts. "Darcy, did you hear me? If you are visiting this morning, you had best get on with it!" When he caught sight of Darcy's expression, he jumped out of his chair and exclaimed, "Good God! What is it? Are you ill? Miss Bennet is surely waiting for your addresses now; I hope you can still go!"

"No, Elizabeth is not waiting for my addresses. She has never wanted them, I am sure. I have done a grave sin in separating Bingley from her sister; it was all arrogance and conceit. I am afraid this has pained her and her family greatly, and I never truly considered that factor. She cannot love me, and I do not deserve her love. I am every part despicable. Please leave me be."

Richard argued against leaving but, after several minutes, agreed to leave Darcy alone with his thoughts. Over the next hour, Darcy's mind began to recover from the blow to his ego and heart. It was a soul-crushing realisation that Elizabeth had not secretly been hoping for his proposal and very likely hated him. All her saucy comments about his pride had been directed to wound. That was how she saw him. He would make amends. It might not ever change her opinion of him, but Darcy knew he had to apologise to her and Bingley. Setting up his writing desk, he confessed his deceit to his friend.

The task of writing to Bingley took until teatime. By then, Darcy had a headache and felt ill. He considered staying in his room because the party from the parsonage was expected to join them. He decided against it, though; he owed Elizabeth an apology.

Mr. and Mrs. Collins arrived along with Miss Lucas, but Elizabeth had stayed behind as she had a headache. Inwardly, Darcy berated himself. Her conversation with Richard must have brought on the illness. Darcy slipped out whilst Lady Catherine held the others' attention over some imagined superiority of hers and Cousin Anne's. The walk to the parsonage went somewhat faster than he expected as he envisioned the upcoming conversation

Too soon, he was at the door, and the maid showed him into the small sitting room. Elizabeth had obviously been crying and had a stack of papers nearby. She looked quite agitated at Darcy's presence. Undoubtedly, she had been rereading letters from her most beloved sister.

Sounding more self-assured than he felt, he finally started with, "Miss Elizabeth, are you well? I heard you were ill with a debilitating headache."

Elizabeth coolly responded, "It is just a headache. *I* will recover."

He immediately sensed her meaning that Jane's heart might not heal from his actions. "I was concerned, truly concerned. My cousin explained you were well this morning. I was alarmed by what could bring on such sudden pain."

"Yes, I was well this morning. I suppose I walked too far or had too much fresh air."

She was obviously reaching for civility; he had never known Elizabeth to complain of overexertion or too much time outside. Determining that he should get on with his purpose as she already knew nearly everything, he took a deep breath. "I believe I owe you an apology. I can see you are upset, and I know it is at my hands. I never wanted to cause you pain. It grieves me that I have been so selfish."

Elizabeth looked confused as she replied, "What can you mean, Mr. Darcy?"

"I was arrogant and selfish to separate Bingley from your sister. If you will, please allow me to explain my motives."

Elizabeth made no answer, and after pausing a moment, Darcy continued speaking. "I was concerned that Bingley would attach himself to a family with no connections or fortune and that, forgive me, lacked propriety. I mistook Bingley's affections for Miss Bennet as no more than his usual flirtations. I can now see that he was, and is, truly attached to her. Likewise, whilst trying to observe your sister for signs of affection, I believed that her heart was not easily touched. I fear now I was mistaken about her character. I have already communicated this grievous error to Bingley, and I hope he will renew his attentions to Miss Bennet. I have informed him that I know she is currently present in London—information which was concealed from him by myself and his sister."

Darcy paced around the room. "At the time, I could not fathom a serious attachment in the place where connection and fortune were lacking. I understood affection but could not comprehend forsaking duties to follow the heart. It has been a hard lesson for me these past months. My advice was also clouded by my eager desire to quickly depart the country because of my own struggle between said affection and duty. It was conceited and arrogant of me to interfere at all, and I certainly had selfish motives as well."

"Oh. I see." Elizabeth paused a moment. "Did you say you recently learned affection was more important than duty?"

To reasons unclear to Darcy, Elizabeth began crying when he nodded. "Dear Elizabeth, I have only made you unhappy again. I had not thought that knowledge would make you so upset."

"No, of course not...it makes perfect sense now. You love Jane." She spoke as though the words caught in her throat.

"What?" Darcy asked incredulously. "No. No, darling. What would make you think that?"

"I have always known you looked at me to criticise and find fault. I did not imagine it was to compare me to Jane. It does make sense, though. At the Meryton Assembly, you said she was the only pretty girl in the room and that I was only tolerable but not tempting enough for a dance. I am a great walker, unladylike at times, and impertinent. Dear Jane is all that is beautiful and good." She took a deep breath and added, "But surely you must know that she is in love with Mr. Bingley."

Darcy was beyond confused as to how Elizabeth could misunderstand his words and meaning so much. He haphazardly stammered, "I...uh...yes, I do know now. I was stupid not to see it earlier, blinded by my own conceit."

This statement served only to cause Elizabeth to forsake intermittent tears for sobs. She buried her face in her hands.

Darcy tried to comfort her with his words. "I can stand this no more. Please stop crying. I cannot bear it."

Elizabeth's cheeks flushed as she dabbed at her eyes with a handkerchief. "Yes, my mother always said men cannot abide to see a woman cry."

Although he vowed not to express his admiration, Darcy could contain himself no longer. "It is you who I love and have loved for many months. I have attempted to subjugate my feelings to no avail."

Elizabeth said nothing, although it was evident to Darcy that he had shocked her. Feeling emboldened, he continued to speak. "First, let me apologise for my unkind words at the Meryton Assembly. I realise now that they have pained you beyond belief. I spoke without even seeing you. I do not like dances in most settings, let alone in a room full of strangers. As you have heard tell, I do not trouble myself with making new acquaintances because I find it very difficult to do so. It has now been many months since I have considered you the handsomest woman of my acquaintance.

"However, it is not only your beauty that has captivated me. Your laughter is the most beautiful music I can hope to hear, your wit is charming, you can find humour in any situation, and you quickly come to the defence of your friends. You never cease to amaze me, and I long for your presence when you are absent. You have haunted my dreams for months now, and I hate myself for causing you such pain and tears. You have bewitched me body and soul. I know I do not deserve it, but I will spend my life making it up to you if you would do me the honour of giving me your hand in marriage."

Elizabeth did not immediately reply. All hope was lost when she did not quickly rejoice at the end of his speech. Now, Darcy only feared why she needed to gather her thoughts before speaking. He readied himself for a lethal blow.

"It is well and good that you seek to make amends now," she began slowly and sadly, "but I wonder at the lack of judgement in a man who made this sort of mistake at all. This is not the only affair I can think of against your character. Mr. Wickham has already explained his mistreatment at your hand. On this subject, what can you have to say?"

Although not surprised at her sentiments over the incident involving her sister, Darcy was taken aback by the accusations flung in his face by Mr. Wickham's treachery. "Why are you so concerned about him?" Dear God, did she love Wickham?

"All who know him feel the same regarding his misfortunes. I am not alone." "His misfortunes!" repeated Darcy.

"You have already deprived him of the best years of his life. You need not treat him with contempt and ridicule as well."

"I need not hear anything else, madam," Darcy said. "You have made your feelings clear. I am sorry for having taken up so much of your time." He hurried out of the room.

While only a few paces from the parsonage, he was surprised to hear Elizabeth call after him. "Mr. Darcy! Pray, do not take such a hasty leave, sir. Perhaps we can continue our discussion inside?"

He slowly turned, barely knowing what he felt at her unexpected words. However, he could hardly trust himself any longer this night. Shaking his head, he began, "No, I have indeed taken up too much of your time. The hour is quite late, and your friends will soon return. It would be better for it not to appear that I called on you alone."

Elizabeth nodded in agreement. "I understand." A gust of wind pulled at a lock of her hair, and she pulled her shawl closer around her shoulders. "I apologise for my reaction. I do not know everything that happened between you and Mr. Wickham, and I should not have brought him up."

Encouraged by her words and reaction, Darcy sought to find another time to meet with her. "I must leave for business on Saturday. I have delayed it long enough. However, I would like to continue this discussion. May I call on you tomorrow?" He tried to hide the desperate sound of hope in his voice.

Elizabeth responded with more timidity than usual. "I should like that." After a moment, she added with more boldness, "I fear I will very much need a walk in the morning and would find company appealing."

Darcy gave her a full smile and strode to her side, taking her hand in his. "Until tomorrow, then," he spoke gently as he raised her hand to his lips, his gaze never leaving her eyes.

He did not know why she had come out to speak with him, but he would not spurn another chance to see her. Indeed, by the time he reached his chamber at Rosings, he had formulated a way to court Elizabeth.

Chapter Four

At the parsonage, nervousness filled Elizabeth with her plans for the day. She was uncertain what made her change her mind about speaking with Darcy again last night. The truth was, she never expected him to realise that his actions affected others or to apologise for them. Even more amazingly, he came to the realisation on his own. His interference with Bingley was kindly meant. She also had to admit she understood how Darcy came to the conclusions that he did regarding Jane. Taking that into consideration, it was probable that Elizabeth might have misunderstood other things about the man. If she were candid with herself, hearing that he loved her and had always admired her cast everything into a new light.

It was now she who owed him an apology. The thought gave her pause on seeing him again, but her courage always rose when afraid, so she would meet Mr. Darcy. Explaining to Charlotte her need for some fresh morning air to help her recover, Elizabeth bid the small party at breakfast adieu until later. Despite her nerves, she found her pace quicker than usual. An unexpected thrill shot up her spine at the image of his tall and firm figure.

"Good morning, Miss Elizabeth," he said as he bowed over her hand. Smiling down at her, he placed her hand on his arm. "You look lovely this morning."

"Thank you and good morning, Mr. Darcy," Elizabeth replied whilst blushing. She had assumed he would be more upset about the nature of this encounter. Instead, he seemed more like a suitor than ever.

"I trust you slept well. Or does your complaint continue?

"I did sleep well. And you, sir?"

She glanced at his face and was intrigued to see the corners of his mouth turning up in a small smile as he replied, "I slept well indeed, Miss Elizabeth."

They lapsed into silence for several minutes until Mr. Darcy cleared his throat. "Miss Elizabeth, last night you alluded to some accusations from Mr. Wickham. Since I do not know the particulars of what he has stated against me, I can offer little refutation. However, I feel as though I should relate to you his dealings with me entirely, instead of merely addressing his accusations."

Elizabeth interrupted him. "Mr. Darcy, there is no need. I beg you, forgive me for saying hurtful words in haste and anger. I was fatigued and emotionally drained. I should not pry into your private affairs. Aside from my complaints about what you said at the assembly in Meryton, I have found you to be an upstanding gentleman, and I am content not to question what must have more than one side and belongs in the past."

He smiled at her words but appeared apprehensive as well. "That is very gracious of you, Miss Elizabeth. But I would have let this knowledge be more generally known had it not been for my selfish pride and fear of harming a dear loved one. I do indeed desire to reveal the truth to you."

Darcy paused for a moment. Before he even began speaking, Elizabeth could see more truth in his look than Wickham had during his tale. Darcy told of his growing up with Wickham and his father's intentions of giving Wickham a valuable living. There is where their stories diverged.

Darcy claimed that Wickham gave up the living in lieu of money. He had already received one thousand pounds upon the reading of the will. Darcy gave him an additional three thousand pounds. Wickham squandered it within months. Some years later, Wickham returned, asking for the living. Darcy could not trust him in a parish and held firm to their original agreement.

Unsurprisingly, Wickham began abusing Darcy's name near and far. If that was not enough, he had attempted to elope with Darcy's young sister last year. No wonder Colonel Fitzwilliam had behaved so strangely when Elizabeth inquired about the girl!

Elizabeth had seen Mr. Darcy in a variety of situations and knew he was no actor. The expressions of pain and remorse he wore whilst speaking were such a contradiction to Wickham's practiced and calm speech. Wickham spoke of not being able to hate Darcy. Elizabeth supposed that if she asked Darcy, he could not promise the same. Perhaps his barely concealed wrath was less palatable to polite society, or ignorant maidens as the case was with herself, but it was far more effective in convincing Elizabeth that Darcy was the injured party.

How differently did everything now appear where Wickham was concerned! His interest in Miss King must only be for her newly acquired ten thousand pounds. Elizabeth braced against a tree as realisation after realisation struck her. She had courted ignorance due to her wounded vanity. Wickham had immediately been pleased with her, and Darcy had not. Therefore, she scrutinised the latter and not the former.

Had she been in love, she could not have been more blind. But vanity, not love, had been her failing. Or had it? Why had she been so upset with Mr. Darcy's first slight against her? She purposefully and wilfully misunderstood nearly everything he had ever said to her. She even argued against the observations of Jane and Charlotte, then twisted the teasing of Colonel Fitzwilliam. Why had the thought of Darcy loving Jane made her cry?

She faced her companion with tears clouding her vision. "Pray, forgive me. I was most wrong about you. I blush in remembrance of my arguments against you last night."

"Miss Bennet, your confusion about my character is understandable. I do not wish for you to censure yourself. There is no need for apologies."

"There most certainly is! If you knew what I said to others, then you would hate me forever."

Darcy stayed their movements and searched her face before meeting her eyes. "I could never hate you, Elizabeth."

Elizabeth stumbled backward, and a surprised gasp left her lips. It was as if she had never seen him before. He truly loved her! She had supposed he simply grew bored with the tedium of Rosings and fancied himself afflicted with love. After another moment of scrutiny, she blushed and lowered her eyes.

"That is very kind of you, Mr. Darcy. However, I know I have done wrong and wish to ask for forgiveness, although I can scarcely hope you will grant it."

Darcy cocked his head to one side. "It is no trouble to forgive you. There was no malice in your words or actions."

"There was." Elizabeth wiped at her eyes. "I wanted to hate you. I wanted to believe the worst about you. I wanted my dislike to be justified."

"Why did you dislike me so much?"

A throaty chuckle erupted, and soon her body shook with laughter. "I can see so clearly now how vain and proud I have been. I only disliked you because I thought you disliked me!"

Shaking his head, Darcy laughed. "We have both been blinded by pride and insecurities. I did not want to like you, I will admit. I came to Hertfordshire with the expectation of finding nothing worthy of my presence. My sole intention was to help Bingley, and although I was loath to go, I desired to assist my friend. It was not many meetings before I realised how impossible it was to ignore you. You tore up my quiet and orderly life, and I craved more."

"You liked me for my impertinence?" Elizabeth's eyes flew to his.

"I admired your lively mind."

"Oh! This proves more than anything how dreadfully wrong I have been about you. If you were truly so proud and of such a hateful nature, then you would never admire that quality in me. I am sure I never spoke to you without the intention to wound."

"And how would you speak to me if that had not been your aim?"

Elizabeth's pulse quickened. They had cleared the air between them. Now that her prejudice did not blind her, where did it leave them?

Elizabeth blushed. "I am unsure. I have never been the recipient of attention from a gentleman of your stature."

"Would you quake in fear of my esteemed personage?"

Laughing, she smiled up at him. She felt something settle in her heart. Darcy had fascinated her for months, but this moment lit a flame. How had she misunderstood her attraction to him? They had quarrelled, but they were making amends. He had earned her respect and esteem and now had her laughing. This was the beginning of intimacy. These were the moments which made a life together.

"Certainly not!" Elizabeth managed to say between giggles. "I suppose I would always have viewed you with suspicion. Perhaps I would have imagined you to be a rake. Why else would you take a fancy to a country gentleman's daughter with no money or connections?"

"Do you truly think so meanly of yourself?"

Elizabeth shrugged. "I do not know that I would persist in that way of thinking. Only it would be one thought which crossed my mind. I would not likely believe you admired me at all. Charlotte has argued the very thing, and I never saw it."

"Perhaps if I had not attempted to hide it."

"And what would your open admiration look like?" She arched one brow, a playful smile on her lips.

Darcy assessed her before replying. "I can be a very determined man, Elizabeth. If I openly courted you, then I would not stop until you were mine."

Elizabeth beamed. "It is too bad you never had the opportunity. Something tells me that would have been a sight to behold."

"May I begin again?"

"You are leaving for London tomorrow."

"Yes, and you will be there in a few weeks."

"I will be staying at Gracechurch Street." Elizabeth lifted her chin and squared her shoulders. "I know you find my relations unworthy of your notice."

"I would be pleased to meet them."

"Would you really?"

"If it would secure your hand, then I would go through any matter of things."

"I cannot be bought." Elizabeth pulled away and began to walk off.

Darcy quickly caught up with her. "I do not mean that you can."

"When I marry, it will be for great love. I will respect my husband. I will not be indebted to him or constantly reminded of the condescension he has shown me by rescuing me from my supposedly low and inferior state."

Darcy caught Elizabeth's hand. "Elizabeth, wait. I would be happy to meet them because they are your family, and you love them. I wish to please you. I desire to show you that I am not so mean as you first believed and am correcting the faults in my character, which you did justly assess. How else could I show you that?"

Elizabeth remained unconvinced and crossed her arms over her chest.

"If you would rather I wait to court you until you return to Longbourn, then I will. If you had hated the idea of my courtship, you would have said so. That can only mean that you are not set against me. I will not quit the field now."

"And manipulating me into loving you is part of your design?"

"No. I wish to share a life with you and everything that means—all of your relations. You should meet mine as well. Together, we would form a family of equal parts yours and mine."

"And your relations would approve of this match?"

"I really do not care."

They were now in view of the parsonage, and Elizabeth saw the curtain of the front sitting room flutter. Discreetly gathering her hand in his, he squeezed it whilst staring into her dark eyes.

"I am yours to command. If you do not wish for me to court you, then tell me so at once. If, however, your feelings have changed, only tell me where and when I may next see you."

Elizabeth took a long moment before replying. All the while, her heart hammered, and her head pounded. She felt as if she were about to jump off a cliff. "Very well, Mr. Darcy. I accept your offer of courtship. I will see you in a fortnight in London." She turned and walked to the parsonage without a backward glance.

Chapter Five

Elizabeth evaded Charlotte's eyes when she entered the parsonage. Too much had happened. She needed to think and breathe before she could say anything to her friend. Making an excuse, she went directly to her room and stayed until dinner. By that point, she had determined she should say nothing to the wife of Lady Catherine's rector. She could hardly be an impartial observer.

Mr. Collins lamented his poor ladyship's misery upon the loss of her nephews. With the way he went on, Elizabeth expected there to be news that Darcy's carriage had met with disaster as soon as it left the park. The thought brought only pain. Just as the thought struck her, Charlotte glanced her way. Elizabeth had to quickly look away lest her friend discover too much.

As Mr. Collins extolled at length his pity for her ladyship, Elizabeth had an excellent excuse for not being her usual self. He made no pause in the conversation, allowing her thoughts to turn to Darcy and their discussion again and again. What man in his senses would wish to court a woman who had already rejected him?

To most men, it would make little difference that Elizabeth's arguments were mostly under false apprehensions. The very fact that he took the time to explain himself illustrated his pride. She no longer felt it was of a sinful sort, but it was there nonetheless. Although he remained determined to win her heart, he did not plead for a second chance.

A little thrill coursed through Elizabeth's body. Her experiences with the other sex had always been less than satisfactory. No man had truly approached as a suitor, save Mr. Collins. He proposed off less than a week's acquaintance, and his speech was so prepared it could have easily been used on any lady. Indeed, his rapid proposal to Charlotte after Elizabeth's refusal was proof enough that he had no attachment to either lady. To marry was to love in his mind. He had made no attempt to woo Elizabeth, and he had refused to accept her rejection.

Darcy offered Elizabeth a choice. He promised that if she allowed him to court her, it would be something for the ages. Whilst she was not usually a senseless romantic, she had to admit that the idea of being the recipient of the regard of an intelligent and powerful man enticed. By the time her head hit the pillow that night, Elizabeth practically vibrated with excitement.

When she awoke, the sun greeted her, and birds sang. After a delightful morning walk, Elizabeth enjoyed the company of Maria and Charlotte. Mr. Collins had gone to Rosings to comfort his patroness. Maria chatted amiably about the expectation to visit Rosings more often and then about the possibilities of London. Elizabeth hid her secret smile as she ducked her head and focused on her needle.

Soon, the post arrived, and with it a letter from Jane. Excusing herself, Elizabeth read in the privacy of her bedchamber.

Dear Elizabeth,

I pray this letter finds you well. I am sure you are enjoying your visit with dear Charlotte no matter the follies of Lady Catherine. You shall not deceive me. I know you find her and the others amusing!

Something most unusual has occurred. You may recall my letter some weeks ago in which I explained that Caroline Bingley did not return my call for many weeks. When at last she appeared at Gracechurch Street, she and Mrs. Hurst stayed for a scant five minutes. It was evident to me that they felt no true friendship for me. I know you had guessed there was duplicity involved, but I would not hear a word against either lady.

Well, today Mr. Bingley called on the house with Caroline in tow. She still did not seem pleased to be present, but she appeared adequately humbled. Mr. Bingley apologised for not visiting earlier. He said something about not being in contact with the parties that knew of my presence in London. I confess it confused me when he said it. However, I shall not borrow misery. Neither shall I hope this means the fruition of my dearest hopes, although he did seem exceptionally happy to see me.

I simply had to tell you, as I cannot explain it to anyone else. Please do not laugh at me, Lizzy. I am determined to allow his actions to be my guide. I will not allow myself to be carried away. I am confident my aunt shall be a more sensible companion than our mother on the matter. I only ask that you be happy for me.

Your loving sister,
Jane

Elizabeth beamed from ear to ear. "I am much mistaken if he is not as in love with you as ever."

She pressed the letter to her heart. Here was proof that Mr. Darcy had written to Bingley. How had he realised his error regarding his friend without speaking to Elizabeth? The fact that he took immediate action to correct his wrong certainly appealed to her.

She quickly wrote a reply to Jane, sharing in her joy and excitement. In addition to Mr. Darcy's courtship, she looked forward to seeing her sister in renewed spirits.

The following day, they were invited to Rosings. Lady Catherine complained so much about the absence of her nephews that Elizabeth wondered if the sole reason why they were asked was to show to them how little she valued them. Among many things said were hints of Darcy's attachment to Rosings, with glances at Miss de Bourgh.

Elizabeth scrutinised Darcy's cousin. He must never have been intended for her if he had proposed to Elizabeth. Miss de Bourgh might have money and an estate, but it did not appear that she ever left Rosings to meet with other gentlemen or to mix in society. Elizabeth could see clearly now that sort of wife would never interest Mr. Darcy.

Most fascinating of all, now that she felt assured of his esteem, Elizabeth discovered she no longer thought so meanly of Miss de Bourgh. Instead, she had compassion for the young lady with an unbearable mother. Elizabeth well understood the pain of that. At least she had sisters and a sensible father. Her family enjoyed the activities of their community. Additionally, they enjoyed friendships with their neighbours. Miss de Bourgh was too high above the villagers to befriend them. Perhaps she and Elizabeth could become more than acquaintances during Elizabeth's remaining weeks in Kent.

"Good evening, Miss de Bourgh," Elizabeth said as they sat at a card table together after dinner.

The lady returned the pleasantry, and Elizabeth's lips twitched as she was reminded of Mr. Darcy's reserve. Perhaps it was a family failing.

"Allow me to extend my apologies about the absence of your cousins. You must miss them."

"Must I?" Miss de Bourgh asked with a smirk.

Perhaps she also shared her sarcastic wit with her cousin. Elizabeth slid a glance at Mr. Collins at the other table before leaning closer to her companion. "Since your cousins are more amiable than mine, I had supposed it to be so, but perhaps I assume too much."

Miss de Bourgh met Elizabeth's eyes and held them before playing her card. "Comparatively speaking, I am sure you are correct. I have the advantage over you, however, in that my cousins are not supercilious and vacant-headed. Additionally, I have a charming female cousin."

"Ah, I have female cousins as well. Alas, they are many years my junior. However, perhaps in time, we shall have more shared companionship. The truth is that Mr. Collins's family is not very close to mine, although I suspect he is attempting to mend that broken fence."

"Is that why he visited you last autumn? Mrs. Collins has mentioned it, and so has my cousin Darcy."

Elizabeth nodded. "He said so in his letter. It seems once he arrived, he had the additional inducement of looking for a wife."

"Ah, and none of his cousins suited him?"

Elizabeth stifled a laugh, something which seemed to give Miss de Bourgh glee. "I could not say. I am excessively happy for my friend and believe she has found a spouse who suits her very well."

"I am sure you are correct. However, I always observed that Mr. Collins was the one who gained the most from the union."

"As you have known him longer than I have, I will bow to your superior knowledge. Although"—Elizabeth leaned in close again— "do not underestimate the value of your mother's advice or the advantages of chickens in my friend's happiness."

Miss de Bourgh finally openly laughed, and Elizabeth felt all the pleasure of having earned what she assumed was not easily given. Mrs. Jenkinson glanced at her charge from where she played cards with Lady Catherine, but Miss de Bourgh waved her off.

"I like you, Miss Bennet," Miss de Bourgh said when she had regained the capacity to speak. "I can see why he does as well."

Elizabeth held her breath at the unspoken mention of Darcy. Had he told his cousin of their recent encounters? She had always supposed him to be a very private man.

"I understand you enjoy reading," Miss de Bourgh said.

The sudden change in conversation left Elizabeth confused, but she replied that she did.

"Excellent. Before you leave this evening, there is a work I should loan you. I believe you will enjoy reading it."

The other table, which had evidently taken their activity more seriously than Elizabeth's, soon ended their game, and Elizabeth was asked to perform on the pianoforte. Elizabeth sighed to herself as the others sat around Lady Catherine as she sermonized on some topic or other. Not for the first time, Elizabeth observed that although her skills were nothing impressive and that, in general, music hindered conversation rather than encouraged it, the request secured Elizabeth in the adjoining room where she could not intrude on the discussion. Undoubtedly, it was all by design so her ladyship could speak without interruption.

As she played this evening, she considered that on her next visit to the estate, she might be met as a niece. What would Lady Catherine's reaction to that be? Her daughter did not seem disappointed by the thought. Whilst Elizabeth had years of experience with silly relatives, she could not say she had many encounters with overbearing ones. Lady Catherine did not intimidate her, but the thought of aligning herself with such an obtrusive and annoying relation did give pause. In the end, Elizabeth dispelled such thoughts. Such things would hardly matter if she were really in love with a gentleman, although she could scarcely suppose that Mr. Darcy would be capable of provoking such a sensation.

Before leaving in the carriage to return to the parsonage, Miss de Bourgh gave Elizabeth the promised book. Upon inspection in her bedchamber, a letter fell out of it.

My Dearest Love,

Are you shocked to receive a letter from me? Forgive me, but I could not bear to wait a fortnight to begin my courtship in earnest. I have discussed the matter with my cousin, and she has agreed to be a courier for us. That is, if you should like to reply. I understand the risks involved in doing so and do not wish to pressure you into anything with which you do not feel comfortable. I have arranged several letters for her to give you regardless of any further communication between us.

I know how much you enjoy walking in the countryside. I confess it is one of the things which attracts me to you the most. I do not enjoy spending much time in London, as I find it too stifling and overpopulated. At my home, or when I visit other counties, I enjoy riding or walking about for exercise as well.

Near Rosings, there is a glen which is a favourite of mine. It is not too far from the lane you favour. If you turn on the footpath near the great oak tree and continue until you see a copse of willows, you shall find it. When you visit, I hope you will think of me. If I were present with you, I would admire the way the sun highlighted your face, bringing out a healthy blush. I would drown in your eyes, brightened by the exercise. I have often imagined seeing the sun on your uncovered hair. I cannot be sure, but I think there may be hues of chestnut among your mahogany tresses. Under the willow trees, I would offer you delectable treats and envy everything you put to your lips.

I know you would tease and laugh at me. In the past, you have assumed I remained mute because I hated the society I was in. What you could not comprehend was that I was rendered dumb by your beauty, grace, and intelligence. Too many times whilst at N— together, I was fascinated by your wit and the rapidity of your mind. The way you challenged me intrigued me. Increasingly, I noted a feeling of disappointment when you chose to end our discussions. I am confident I even felt jealous of my dearest friend when you came to his defence one evening. Once in London, I realised what my heart had been whispering in H—. My heart had found what it was searching for, and no one else would do.

When I see you next, I will attempt to moderate my stupidity. However, do not be surprised if I am overcome with admiration once more. I fear, my beloved, that it may be many more meetings before I can put aside my appreciation of you enough to speak openly. I am hardly at ease doing so in any environment, and as I shall call on you at G— Street, I did not want you to misunderstand the nature of my behaviour.

To this reason, I intend to call on your relations before your arrival. I believe Mr. B shall renew his attentions to your sister, and I will accompany him there on occasion. Although I am uncomfortable with new acquaintances, I will make every effort to become their friend. I do this not to change your opinion of me but because I have an acquaintance in London, and I should visit her. There is the added inducement of hoping I shall be over my nerves by the time of your arrival. However, regardless of how comfortable I feel in your aunt's drawing room, I cannot promise that I will be able to do more than drink in the sight of you. I hope this does not offend.

Yours always and affectionately...

*****

The following morning, Elizabeth took the path described by Darcy. When she reached the glen, she smiled at the view. She could see why he would enjoy this area. It was secluded. A private space for a private man.

Would she return communications with him? It was quite the risk. If they were exposed, her reputation could be ruined. Oh, Darcy would surely offer marriage again—but did she wish for that? Only a few days ago she had thought him the last man in the world she would be willing to marry.

Elizabeth shook her head. Perhaps that was a little hyperbolic. At certain times, he might have been the last, such as just after she gathered from Colonel Fitzwilliam that Darcy had separated Bingley and Jane. However, most of the time, Darcy was merely annoying or a source of amusement. Surely there were worse men in the world. She would have preferred the haughty and annoying man from Derbyshire over Mr. Collins.

No, she did not wish to marry Darcy at present. She was unsure if they could truly be friends, with their past and his present feelings. The only way to know him better was to either accept his courtship or rebuff him entirely when he had asked to court her in London. She did not need to decide at present, but surely, he would want a definitive answer when she arrived in town. While she could terminate their arrangement at any moment without damage to her reputation, she did not think it was kind to trifle with his feelings. When she accepted seeing him in London, she had not anticipated he would court her from afar. However, now that he was doing so, she had the opportunity to determine her feelings before reaching town. Once there she would need to tell him if he had any hope of obtaining her hand in marriage.

Thoughts of London turned her mind to acknowledging how he had righted his wrong against Jane. It said very much about Darcy's character that he took measures to tell Bingley of his deviousness. Drawing her knees up to her chin, Elizabeth wrapped her arms around her legs as she thought. The fact that Darcy could use such arts at all said nothing good about him. She had always supposed right and wrong were as clearly distinct as black and white. However, perhaps they were more like night and day. There were moments when you were not quite sure of the hour. The haze of dusk and dawn left one confused. The only sure fit was to wait and see. That was all she could do at present. The truth always came out in the end.

Chapter Six

Darcy read over Anne's letter with a frown. Elizabeth had sent no messages to him. He had assumed she would not—at least not right away—and yet he could not prevent the disappointment which tugged at his heart. Wooing her in person might assuage some of his longings, but he was unsure it was the best way to allow her to change her opinion of him. She needed time to see him in a different light, and nothing showed the change in one person better than absence.

A knock interrupted his thoughts, and Bingley was shown into his study. "Are you ready to leave?"

Darcy smiled at his friend. Bingley had been angered by Darcy's deceit. However, it only lasted until he had seen Miss Bennet once more. He reserved far more anger for his sister, who had not only concealed Miss Bennet's visit but also treated her shabbily. Darcy had not suggested that to Miss Bingley, but in truth, he might have. Elizabeth showed him that he was not above being rude and impolite when it served his purposes.

"Of course." Darcy rose from his seat. "I look forward to meeting the Gardiners."

"You will be quite impressed with them," Bingley said with a grin. "They are nothing like Mrs. Bennet or her sister. I think even you will see it must be where Jane and Miss Elizabeth get their grace and intelligence."

Darcy chose not to correct his friend on the impropriety of calling Miss Bennet by her Christian name. It was not as though he did not do the same with Elizabeth and he had no encouragement from her. Nor were Bingley's intentions any secret from Darcy. A shred of insecurity nipped at the back of his mind. This was another connection to Elizabeth, and should she refuse him again, it would be another tie he must break or bear to see her through. It added to his anxiety, but he would repress it. He would conquer it to do what was right. They were worthy of his esteem, and Miss Bennet was his acquaintance. He should call on her in any case, but how could he refuse the request of his closest friend? He would do what a true gentleman did and put the needs of others above his own.

An hour later, Darcy left the Gracechurch Street abode of Mr. and Mrs. Gardiner with a smile on his face. Bingley clapped him on the back. "You can breathe now, Darcy. I told you there was nothing to fear. The Gardiners are very respectable, and Jane would never hold a grudge."

Darcy nodded, although it was not the eldest Miss Bennet he had worried about.

"I have never understood why you and Caroline detested the Gardiners so much when I have ties to trade as well," Bingley said once the carriage was moving.

"I cannot speak for your sister," Darcy said, "but I never disliked the Gardiners on the principle that they were from trade. Your ties are not as strong as one who actively pursues the profession, of course. I am uncertain I ever thought of the Gardiners at all."

Bingley gave Darcy an incredulous look. "Do not lie to me. You pointed out Miss Bennet's low connections to me just as well as Caroline did. I am certain it must be why you never acted on your attraction to Miss Elizabeth."

"My what?" Darcy sputtered. He had not thought others noticed his admiration.

"Do not be so surprised." Bingley laughed. "Caroline was not the only one to see how you were with Miss Elizabeth. I have never known you to spend so much time staring at a lady, let alone speaking with her! You fancied her; admit it."

Darcy sighed, tired of the facade and knowing that he had promised Elizabeth to court her in truth when she arrived in London. "Very well." Darcy nodded. "I ardently admire Elizabeth."

"And?" Bingley leaned forward with an expectant and eager look. "I know you saw her in Kent."

"And I have plans to ask for her hand in marriage."

"Indeed!" Bingley sat back, astonished. Then a troubled look passed over his face. "Darcy...I do not know how to tell you but..."

"She does not like me?" Darcy stared out a window as he said it. The less pain Bingley saw him express, the better.

"If you know that, then I am confused as to why you wish to marry her."

"It cannot be helped. It is a foolish cause, but it would be more foolish not to propose to the lady whom I love."

"Love!" Bingley cried in amazement.

Darcy swung his head to his friend. "Why else would I want to marry her? You have said it yourself: her connections can do nothing for me. Not that I ever considered that very much anyway. If I had, I would have married years ago."

"Yes, I suppose your cousin has been waiting in the wings for you."

Darcy laughed. "You suppose incorrectly. She has been in love with my cousin Richard, only he is too stupid to notice."

"Is that right?" Bingley joined in the laughter. "I am curious how you know Miss Elizabeth dislikes you. You did not seem very aware of the fact in Hertfordshire."

"As you say, we saw one another in Kent."

"And?" Bingley leaned forward once again.

"Those big brown eyes might work on the ladies, but you will not charm me."

"I should hope not!" Bingley chuckled and sat back. "By the by, men and women marry for reasons other than love and wealth. Mutual attraction comes to mind, and that you and Elizabeth have in spades."

"I thought you said she did not like me?" Darcy could not help it. Every muscle in his body snapped to attention with the intimation that Elizabeth was attracted to him.

"She might not have liked you, but she could not keep her eyes from you either. She always commanded your notice and put herself forward to garner it. Of course, Caroline called it much more vulgar things. Elizabeth is no green miss. She had to know what she was doing."

"What are you saying?" Darcy's voice had a hard edge to it. If Bingley were saying he was duped by Elizabeth or that she was free with her favours, he would have a hard time not calling him out, friend or not.

Bingley raised his hands. "Only that she might not have understood her fascination, but she was fascinated all the same. That is quite a lot to build a marriage upon. I know of several couples who, after they have four or five children in the same number of years, come to realise they love each other."

Darcy rolled his eyes. "I would suppose you might know even more couples who come to realise after a year or two of slaking their lust that they do not love each other."

Bingley shrugged. "What is your plan, then? You must want her to love you."

Darcy clenched his fists as his heart galloped at the thought. That was his dearest wish. "Our courtship begins in earnest when she arrives in London. However, I am not above pressing my advantage. I may be absent from Rosings, but I have arranged for my cousin to be a courier for various messages and gifts."

"You are breaking propriety?"

"Not very much." Darcy smirked. "I would never endanger her reputation. They are not gifts which would require an explanation to others and draw their suspicion."

"Such as?"

Darcy eagerly told Bingley of the encounter he had arranged for Elizabeth the other day. When he finished, Bingley whistled. "I would be half in love with you after a letter like that."

Bingley batted his eyes, and Darcy rolled his. "Spare me your antics. I am certain it will take far more effort to earn Elizabeth's love."

"What are your next plans for her?"

"Anne is to invite Elizabeth to Rosings whilst Mrs. Collins and her sister work in the parish. During their time together, they will visit my aunt's bird conservatory. Select species will have messages attached to their legs."

"Messages?"

"Bits of poetry which remind me of her. I thought it would not be unusual for Anne to copy poetry."

"What does your cousin get out of all of this?"

"Ah," Darcy said, "I will suggest to her mother that she ought to come to London to visit Georgiana. Lady Catherine will agree, as she wishes to see me wed her daughter. Anne hopes to come and attempt to work her way into Richard's heart."

"I begin to see how you could deceive me about Jane."

"Allow me to apologise again. I had no mean intentions. It was foolish and officious of me to interfere. Affairs of the heart are never a secure endeavour, and I ought to have trusted you knew what you were about."

"I accept your unnecessary second apology. I know the intrusion was well-meant, and you only wished to care for me." Bingley raised his brows. "Does Miss Elizabeth know about this?"

"Yes." Darcy grunted and fell silent for a moment as memories of her righteous anger washed over him.

"Have you told her that you have made amends?"

"I would not want to boast."

"It never stopped you before." Bingley laughed.

Darcy scrunched his face up. Had he been boastful in the past? He never took pains to conceal his attributes. He was not as modest as Bingley, but was he boastful? "I apologise if that is so."

"I am only teasing," Bingley assured him. "You are proud, but you do not boast about yourself. If you did, then Elizabeth would already think better of you."

They arrived at Darcy House, where they greeted Georgiana and enjoyed refreshments before Bingley left for the day. They would see each other again at the Gardiner residence in a few days, as they had both been invited to dine with them.

Georgiana followed Darcy to his study. "Is the Miss Bennet who is currently in London the same as the one who stayed at Netherfield last autumn?"

"Yes." Darcy nodded as he sat behind the desk. "She is the eldest sister. The one who was ill, if you recall from my letters."

"Oh, so she is not the sister who walked through the mud?"

"Did I include that detail?"

"You certainly did."

"How interesting that you remember my correspondence better than I. What is your reason for forgetting to call on your aunt and uncle or practice your French?"

Georgiana huffed. "It is easy to forget an unenjoyable practice, but you seldom write to me about a young lady."

"Why do you ask about Miss Bennet?" Darcy felt he was treading on dangerous ground. He did not wish to say more to his sister about Elizabeth at present.

"I feared Mr. Bingley and you fancied the same lady, and that was why you returned to London so suddenly, avoided him most of the winter, were listless and morose, and then stayed in Kent longer than originally planned."

Darcy blinked at his sister. "How do you expect me to respond to such assumptions?"

"Oh, denial, of course."

Shaking his head, Darcy motioned for his sister to sit on the opposite side of his desk. "I am not interested in Bingley's lady."

"But you are interested in a lady?" Her face lit with joy and then immediately fell.

"Does the thought pain you?" He had not taken into consideration that his sister might not like Elizabeth or any lady he courted.

"I suppose it would depend on the lady," she answered neutrally.

"Are there any who specifically worry you?"

"Dozens, but our cousin and Miss Bingley are at the top of the list."

"Why is that?" He hoped to put her off the subject of ladies he did fancy.

"They are all wrong for you."

"I thought they were your friends."

"They are." Georgiana nodded. "However, Miss Bingley would be too domineering. She would care only for your wealth. The same would be said of countless other ladies, but I fear she has the greatest advantage due to your friendship with her brother." Georgiana feigned absentmindedness and toyed with the fringe on her shawl. "On the other hand, I adore Anne...but she is not for you."

Darcy smirked. "You mean I am not for her."

She immediately stilled. "What do you know?"

"Anne is in love with Richard."

"Do you have insights into his heart?"

Darcy shook his head. They never spoke on such things. With the way Richard had flirted with Elizabeth, he doubted Richard favoured Anne or ever would.

There was a knock on the door, and Darcy checked his watch. It must be Georgiana's music instructor. His sister's mouth fell open.

"Oh!" she cried. "You put me off the topic on purpose! Now, do not think I will forget. We have not had the last on this subject."

The butler knocked and announced that Miss Darcy was requested in the music room to begin her lesson. Darcy breathed a sigh of relief when she had left. He did not think he could put her off forever, but he did not believe Elizabeth would want him discussing courtship plans with a stranger to her. Soon, he hoped, everything would be public. Soon.

Chapter Seven

Elizabeth smiled as she looked at the stream before her. Darcy had arranged another outing for her in the surroundings of Rosings. She laughed to herself. She really ought to have known better than to think he would wait until she arrived in London to court her. He was a man used to getting his every whim and pressing his advantage.

Over a week had passed since their last formal conversation. However, Darcy communicated with her daily. Elizabeth still refused to write to him directly, and she was far too private a person to give any secret messages to Anne. He would simply have to bear the burden of not knowing the change of her heart for a few more days. It was a pain of his own making, after all. Elizabeth shook her head, thinking of how she would tease him about it when they were reunited.

She had not wanted to fall in love with Mr. Darcy and certainly did not dream it would happen so fast. Once free of her false perceptions and seeing proof of his superior character and ardent love, it was all too easy to let her heart begin to hope. In truth, he was the sort of man she had always wished to someday marry. Mr. Darcy was intelligent, thoughtful, sensitive, loving, and well-respected. She even saw his flaws in a new light. His once hideous pride was now proof that he cared for his family legacy. His interference with Jane, although she had not entirely learned to justify or excuse him, was proof of his extreme loyalty.

"What surprise do you have for me today, Fitzwilliam?" Elizabeth had taken to calling Darcy by his Christian name when alone and speaking aloud as though he were present.

Shading her eyes from the morning's rays, Elizabeth saw a glass bottle in the stream. She followed the rope around it to the low branch of a nearby tree and eagerly pulled forth her treasure. Popping the cork, she found a tightly rolled piece of paper in the now familiar hand of Mr. Darcy.

To My Beloved,

I count the days until I may see you again. I have waited my whole life to share the world with the woman I love at my side. I hope you will not keep me waiting long after we are reunited. However, I do not mean to rush you. I will wait patiently for you.

Elizabeth laughed and shook her head. No, he would not. He might not push her, but Darcy would not sit passively and idle either. Then again, she would not have wanted him to do so.

Did you attempt to count the stars last night as I requested in my most recent missive? They are as endless as my love for you, and your eyes shine even brighter than the celestial orbs. As long as I live, a night-time sky will remind me of your smiling face and enchanting eyes.

If you feel up to a dare, then skip rocks whilst you tell me of your favourite books. When I see you next, I want to hear all about it. See if you can best my childhood record of six skips or my cousin's eight. Be sure to destroy this letter, as I would hate for there to be written proof that he was ever better than me at anything.

With my enduring love...

Elizabeth sighed at the finish. Darcy did not sign his name to these letters. He could not, lest they enter the wrong hands or she be found with them. He always reminded her of his enduring love in the closing. Not too long ago, she would have questioned whether any man were capable of such a feat. However, Jane's letters glowed with joy in her reunion with Bingley. In the letter Elizabeth received yesterday, Jane revealed that Bingley had proposed, and she had accepted. Bingley's love was not diminished at all in the months since seeing Jane at Hertfordshire. And according to Darcy, his passion for Elizabeth had only grown since leaving Netherfield. Surely he could manage a fortnight.

"I want to see you," she murmured to herself. She scooped up ten pebbles ideal for skipping and told her imaginary companion all about her reading preferences. The sun was high in the sky when she determined she must leave her private sanctuary. She retired early that evening under the guise of fatigue from the morning, and she wrote her own missives which would be handed over to Darcy when they next met. He shared so much of his heart and his feelings that she felt it was only right to reciprocate.

Console Colonel Fitzwilliam as best you can when you tell him I broke his record and skipped ten rocks today.

I can hardly wait to see you and be courted in truth. I think I understand now what my heart always felt since first meeting you. It has taken me so long to see the truth. I used to think highly of my wit and intelligence, but how did I deceive myself so? What other reason could there be for my heart to beat more rapidly when your name is mentioned? Why did I always know when you were looking my way? Why do you provoke me so much?

It can only be love.

I love you, my darling Fitzwilliam.

As she would hand the letters to Darcy in person, she felt no need to omit names. Elizabeth sealed the letter with wax and placed a kiss on it. Soon, very soon, she hoped to replace the sensation with Darcy's lips. The thought of his kisses and tender caresses made her feel lightheaded and giddy as she readied for bed. "Soon," she whispered to herself.

******

"I can hardly believe Lady Catherine is sending us to London in her best carriage," Maria Lucas said as she boarded the coach.

"Yes, Mother wanted us to ride in style," Anne said with a knowing smile for her companions. "I am so thankful to have met you, Elizabeth, and you as well, Miss Lucas. I have been asking Mother to allow me to visit London without her for years."

Anne and Elizabeth shared a glance. It had not all been quiet moments of concealed courtship in Elizabeth's last fortnight in Kent. She had developed a friendship with Miss de Bourgh, and the two now called one another by their first names. In one of their arranged meetings, Elizabeth learned that Anne had long loved her cousin Richard. The relief Elizabeth felt at knowing Anne was not a rival for Darcy's affections was the first clue that she felt more for the gentleman than she had previously thought.

"Where will we change horses?" Maria asked as she looked out a window at the passing countryside.

"Mother has arranged for us to stop at The Chaise and Four in Bromley."

Elizabeth hid a secret smile. In one of her missives from Darcy, he had confessed to favouring a different inn at Bromley. He claimed it had the best Toad in the Hole he had ever eaten. Elizabeth had laughed for nearly five whole minutes at the image of the stern and arrogant Mr. Darcy she used to know enjoying a peasant's meal. The information would thoroughly scandalise his aunt and Miss Bingley! If all went well, she could sample the fare next year on her trip to Rosings. She and Anne would be real cousins by then.

"I am surprised you are not sadder to leave Kent, Eliza," Maria observed.

"I shall surely miss Charlotte, and there are many beautiful surroundings, but I immensely look forward to London." Elizabeth could barely contain her glee. She would arrive too late in the day to see Darcy tonight, but tomorrow he would call at Gracechurch Street.

"I had thought you would miss the long walks you had at Rosings. I noticed you were gone for long periods every morning and seemed happier than I am used to seeing you at Longbourn."

"Perhaps it is the novelty of a holiday which created such enjoyment," Anne said, quickly rescuing Elizabeth.

"Indeed." Elizabeth nodded. "I think you must be correct. In any case, I have dearly missed my sisters, especially Jane. I am most eager to arrive at the Gardiners' house."

"Your aunt and uncle are very kind to host me for the few days we will be in London." Maria beamed at Elizabeth. She was part of a large family and had seldom stayed in town.

"They are most happy to do so," Elizabeth assured her friend's sister.

The conversation soon turned to other matters, with Mrs. Jenkinson, Anne's companion, adding commentary now and then. Elizabeth's mind wandered. A thousand anxieties and worries fluttered in her mind. Had she built Darcy up too high in her head? Could his love remain true despite her flaws? During the winter, he had imagined her to be nearly perfect. Courting from a distance was quite a different matter than courting in person. Could he really tolerate her low connections?

Would his family object too much to the match? Would his friends?

Finally, they reached Gracechurch Street. Anne declined to come in, as she was fatigued from the journey, but promised to call soon. Reunited with Jane, Elizabeth's thoughts of Darcy momentarily fled. She was pleased to see her sister in excellent health and spirits. Her joy overflowed and was evident in her countenance and every look and gesture. They had just missed Mr. Bingley, who often arrived during breakfast and stayed through the morning.

The remainder of the day was full of time with the Gardiners and their children. At last, Elizabeth and Jane retired for the evening. As Maria stayed in a different chamber, the sisters were finally alone.

"Tell me, truly," Elizabeth began as she took Jane's hands in hers, "are you as happy as you look?"

"Oh, Lizzy!" Jane cried. "I could not have imagined such happiness. I am beyond blessed and only wish for all my family and friends to know the joy and good fortune that I have."

"You deserve every wonderful thing, and no man less agreeable than Mr. Bingley would have been worthy of your hand. I can hardly wait to call him brother."

"Speaking of brothers, I think I might call a certain young man one before too long."

Elizabeth feigned shock. "What, is someone courting Mary or Kitty? Surely Lydia is far too young."

"Do be serious," Jane said with a smile which proclaimed she was not put out with Elizabeth's tease. "I mean Mr. Darcy will marry you, of course."

"Will he? That is quite news to me!"

Jane furrowed her brow. "I do not understand. Bingley said enough for me to understand that Darcy greatly admires you. He has visited Gracechurch Street several times since his return to London. I know you did not like him in Hertfordshire, but surely his visits here are proof enough of his good nature. It would be an excellent match. You are very well suited to one another."

"You know that I have always wished for love," Elizabeth murmured. She could not voice her feelings to Jane before she spoke to Darcy.

"Can you not learn to love him?"

She had learned to love him. However, she had previously hated him. How could she be certain her feelings would not change again? How could she be sure his would not alter? It was far too soon to speak of such things.

Jane interrupted Elizabeth's thoughts. "I believe he is to call on us tomorrow. There will be time enough to see what may happen. Bingley is soon to return to Netherfield, and surely Darcy will visit as well. Once I marry, you can stay with me and often be thrown in his path."

Elizabeth laughed. "Goodness! You sound like Miss Bingley — or Mama!"

"I hope I never sound like Caroline." Jane made a face.

"Bravo! I did not think you could think ill of a person."

"I know she only acted in the best interest of her brother, but she did not have to feign being my friend for so long or so well. I have forgiven her, but I will not forget it and be too eager to trust her again."

Elizabeth twisted her hands. If Bingley had implicated his sister in their separation, had he said anything of Darcy's role? Could Jane forgive him? "You did not fully explain in your letter how Mr. Bingley never knew you were in town."

Jane sighed before explaining to Elizabeth that Caroline had intentionally kept the information from her brother. "I know Mr. Darcy also counselled against Bingley's return to Netherfield. Bingley even confessed that Darcy knew I was in town and said nothing to his friend."

Elizabeth sucked in a breath. "How do you feel about that?"

"Mr. Darcy has apologised to me, and I have forgiven him. I see quite a difference between his actions and Caroline's. Bingley, too, bears some blame. However, none of us are perfect, and I should hope not to be judged only by my errors."

Elizabeth applauded her sister for her good sense and loving heart, all the while realising how much wiser Jane was than she. The hour had grown late, and they elected to sleep.

The following morning, Elizabeth awoke before Jane. She could hardly contain her nerves at seeing Darcy again. One moment she looked forward to the encounter; the next she feared it. In the past, he had always relied on her to carry the conversation. Now, she felt too anxious to formulate two coherent sentences.

She barely touched her breakfast, drawing concerned looks from her aunt.

Visiting hours came and went without Darcy. Bingley had arrived at his usual time and confirmed that when he had last seen Darcy, he had planned on calling that morning. He awkwardly guessed aloud that something dire must have occurred to keep him away. Elizabeth hardly knew what to think. Why had Darcy not come? If he were detained, he might have sent a note to Mrs. Gardiner or even have Anne write to Elizabeth.

A feeling of dread filled the pit of Elizabeth's stomach. She had rejected his first, and perhaps only, proposal. She had declined the opportunity to write to him whilst she remained in Kent. All his notes to her were arranged before he had left. Had a fortnight in London made him forget about Elizabeth? She had thought at first that he only fancied himself in love due to the boredom of Rosings. He claimed to have loved her for many months — and yet he had not acted on that love. Perhaps he now avoided her to lessen his attachment.

Elizabeth's heart whispered that he still loved her. However, her head doubted that a man as sensible and admirable as he would desire to marry a woman with such flawed thinking and who had previously spurned him.

She continued to wrestle with the thoughts all day and long into the night. As silent tears soaked into her pillow, she whispered, "Why did you not come, Fitzwilliam?"

Chapter Eight

The next morning, Anne called at Gracechurch Street. She brought Miss Darcy with her, but not Mr. Darcy. Although she had tried not to give clues about her feelings, Elizabeth knew her disappointment was evident in her features when the two ladies entered the Gardiners' drawing room.

Miss Darcy was a delightful young lady. Mr. Wickham had called her proud, but Elizabeth quickly saw she was timid. Of course, it was not the first lie Mr. Wickham had told. Elizabeth cringed for ever believing him and knew it might have cost her Darcy's esteem.

Once Mrs. Gardiner had Miss Darcy, Maria, and Jane sufficiently involved in a conversation, Anne turned her attention to Elizabeth. "Darcy was not at home when I arrived. It seems he hurriedly left the day before our arrival, but no one knows where. He called for his horse and hastily packed a few items for saddlebags. He offered no information about his direction and had only promised that he would return soon."

Elizabeth chewed her bottom lip. It did not seem as though he intended to journey all the way to Pemberley.

However, the fact that he left no note for her and intentionally missed her arrival confirmed her deepest fears. "He knew he would not be present for my arrival in London."

Anne squeezed Elizabeth's hand. "I am sorry, but it appears so. Do not give up on him yet. There might be a reasonable explanation for it all."

"I am sure there is." Elizabeth nodded. "What could be more reasonable than to serve me my just desserts. How heartily I regret every saucy speech I gave him!"

"I do not think it possible that he intentionally engaged your heart just to humble you and make you regret him. He has too much honour for that. Indeed, if he believed your heart attached, he would feel compelled to offer for you even if he no longer loves you."

"I am sure you are correct. He must believe me capable of changing my opinion on a whim. If he stays away for a week, then perhaps I might give up on him entirely. After all, the last he heard from me, I barely welcomed his courtship at all."

"I think that sort of art is too close to deceit for my cousin. He would use more honourable means to make his disinterest known."

Elizabeth shrugged. She did not wish to explain to Anne about Darcy's interference with Jane and Bingley. It was done with good intentions, but it was deceitful all the same. He was not above such things when he thought it for the best. She could not blame him in the least. He must have no desire to be reminded of his past love for her or to recall her previous abuse of him.

Anne and Miss Darcy could not stay for long. Another two days passed without much change at the Gardiner residence. Bingley arrived at breakfast and stayed through morning calls. Sometimes he took Jane for a drive around Hyde Park, and Elizabeth was invited as a chaperone. Once they went to the theatre. In every crowd, Elizabeth searched for Darcy's familiar features. It seemed most unusual that he would not communicate with his family and friends. However, perhaps they were sworn to secrecy.

On the fifth day after her arrival in London, Elizabeth withdrew a box from her trunk. It contained the various missives and scraps of information she had garnered from Darcy. There were snippets of poetry, letters of love, a childhood story, even an entry from his journal from before his arrival at Rosings in which he confessed his love for her. How could the man who gave her all these things now be avoiding her and have forgotten all about her? How could he awaken such love in her heart only to separate himself from her forever?

Elizabeth stared down at the heartfelt words in her hands through the tears in her eyes. She had thought she loved him—really, truly loved him. She thought she understood his mind, nay, his heart. Mere days ago, she was more confident than the next breath that he loved her. Why should she doubt him because of an unexplained absence? Perhaps she ought to worry for him rather than about his love.

Wiping her eyes, Elizabeth put the items back in her keepsake box. Clutching it to her heart, she ran down the stairs to find her aunt. A scan of the room proved

Maria was upstairs and Elizabeth could be assured of relative secrecy as she spilled her heart to her aunt and sister. "Aunt, I wish to call on Darcy House at once."

Mrs. Gardiner snapped her head up from her sewing but only blinked at her niece for a moment. Her mouth opened and closed in several attempts to speak, but no sound came out. She looked at Jane for help.

"Lizzy, are you unwell?" Jane put down her work and came to Elizabeth's side, eyeing her with concern.

"I am extremely well, but Mr. Darcy may not be."

"You have been crying." Mrs. Gardiner's words left no room for doubt.

"Yes, but I finally see things clearly. Please, we must hurry."

"Elizabeth," Mrs. Gardiner began and then motioned for her niece to come to her side. Once seated next to her, she gathered Elizabeth's hands in hers. "Why do you wish to call on Darcy House? It is most unseemly—"

"Anne and I are good friends," Elizabeth interjected. "She and Miss Darcy recently called here, and we may return the call with impunity. However, there is something wrong with Mr. Darcy. I know it!"

Mrs. Gardiner frowned. "He is his own man, my darling. If he does not wish to pay his respects to you, no one can force him. I am sorry to say it, and I had thought highly of him, but young men often get over these flirtations, and young ladies often make too much of them."

"When you first met him, did you think he admired me?"

"It was not immediately obvious; however, your uncle and I thought we detected some partiality."

"There was. He loved me then and had said as much in Kent. He loves me still!"

"How can you be sure?" Jane asked, her eyes cast down.

"He courted me at Rosings." Elizabeth held up her box of treasures. "This is full of the tokens he sent me. I know his mind, and more importantly, I know his heart. We must convince Darcy's family to mount a search."

"Even if we did that, where would they start?" Mrs. Gardiner asked.

"There must be some indication of where he went," Elizabeth said. "If I am mistaken and he is merely avoiding me, then I will bear the weight of my foolishness. Do not waste time worrying over my reaction or wondering about my senses, for nothing shall shake me from this. I will go unchaperoned in a hack if I must."

Mrs. Gardiner and Jane shared a look which appeared to Elizabeth to be full of doubt, pity, and caution. At last, Mrs. Gardiner stood and said, "Very well. Allow me to inform the governess and Miss Lucas. Fetch your outdoor clothes."

On the ride to Mayfair, Elizabeth ignored the questioning looks of her aunt and sister. The Mr. Darcy she knew would never disappear for days without so much as telling his sister. He would never let Anne down when he had arranged for her to come to London. She did not think Miss Darcy could lie so well, and

Anne had no reason to do so. Mr. Darcy was not hiding in his townhouse.

Arriving at Darcy House, they were shown to a spacious drawing room where Anne, Georgiana, and their companions awaited them. Before they could be seated, Colonel Fitzwilliam was announced.

"Anne, Georgie, what do you mean Darcy is missing?" he began as soon as he entered without looking at the occupants.

"Oh! You are worried about Mr. Darcy, too?" Elizabeth cried, relief and worry mixed in her voice.

"Pardon me. I did not see you had guests." Colonel Fitzwilliam turned from his cousins to Elizabeth. "Miss Bennet! I did not expect to see you here! Does everyone know Darcy is missing but me?"

"Perhaps it would be best if we introduced everyone and allowed our guests to sit," Mrs. Annesley suggested.

Once formal introductions were made, Elizabeth looked nervously from one Darcy cousin to the next. Seated next to one another, she quickly saw the familial resemblance. She had not expected to have to make her case to Colonel Fitzwilliam immediately. Butterflies filled her stomach.

Elizabeth cleared her throat. "I had expected Mr. Darcy to call on me the morning after I arrived in London. That was five days ago. Anne and Miss Darcy explained that Mr. Darcy left without a word the day before our arrival. I believe it is rather uncharacteristic of him to go so long without communicating his whereabouts to his sister."

"Indeed, most out of character," Colonel Fitzwilliam agreed. "However, sometimes a man might prefer to make himself scarce." He gave Elizabeth a knowing look, causing her to wince.

"I do not understand," Georgiana said. "Why would Fitzwilliam prefer to hide himself away somewhere?"

Colonel Fitzwilliam coughed and then rubbed the back of his neck. "I should not expose my cousin's secrets, even to his sister. Suffice it to say that a man may have several reasons he does not wish to be in the company of a certain lady."

"You mean when he wants to discourage her affection," Anne said, her brows rising in a challenge.

Richard assessed her for a moment. "Or when he desires to discourage his own."

Georgiana huffed and crossed her arms over her chest. "Is it that you think Fitzwilliam does not want Miss Elizabeth to love him, or is it that you think he does not want to love her?"

"Georgie!" Anne and Richard exclaimed in unison.

"My dear, sometimes it is better to be a little less direct," Mrs. Annesley said with a pat on her charge's knee.

"I do not see what I said was wrong. We are attempting to settle if my brother is missing or only a coward. If he is missing, it has been nigh on a week and we have lost precious time. For myself, I know he fancied a lady, and I believe it was Miss Elizabeth."

Elizabeth looked at Anne but was surprised to hear Colonel Fitzwilliam speak instead. "Yes, he once thought to propose to her, but we left Rosings without news of an engagement. Therefore, I presume the lady does not return his affections. Why did you expect Darcy to call on you, Miss Elizabeth?"

Before Elizabeth could reply, Anne interrupted. "You spoke from knowing Darcy's feelings and not out of your own experience? Will any man hide away from a lady to kill his affection or only Darcy?"

"What?" Colonel Fitzwilliam sputtered. "Why, surely I am speaking of Darcy."

Anne raised her brows as a pleased smile crossed her face. "Do you know that ladies sometimes do the same thing?"

"If we might get back to the issue of my brother being missing," Georgiana said in a clipped voice.

Elizabeth's head swirled with the mix of so many strong personalities. Perhaps this is how Darcy felt when he met the Bennets! "I know Mr. Darcy loves me. Although I did not accept his proposal, I agreed to a courtship. It was supposed to begin when I returned to London, but he arranged for various letters to be sent to me through Anne."

"If you expected him to call on you the very first day, why have you waited until now to worry about his absence?" Colonel Fitzwilliam asked.

Elizabeth lowered her eyes. "I feared he might have changed his mind. I gave him ample reason to do so."

"Yes, men are much fickler with their hearts than ladies are," Anne agreed.

"Not all men," Colonel Fitzwilliam countered. "As it happens, I know that Darcy pined for you for months,

Miss Elizabeth. I do not think anything could end his love for you."

"Perhaps he thought better of the match, even if he still loved you," Georgiana suggested.

Elizabeth nodded. "I feared that as well. I am not a simpleton. I know he gains nothing by wedding me. However, after wrestling with my insecurities for days, I listened to my heart. I know he still loves me, and something has befallen him. If he no longer wished to court me, he would have enough honour to inform me. He certainly would not conceal his location from his family, especially Miss Darcy."

"If he is missing, and that is quite a big if, I might add," Richard said, "where do you propose we begin?"

"He did not take a carriage or his valet," Georgiana explained. "He told the staff he would return in a day or two."

"That does limit the distance from London, but we have no idea in which direction to begin the search."

"I would suggest he went to Kent," an unexpected voice from the doorway said. Elizabeth turned to see Mr. Bingley. "Pardon me. I arrived at Gracechurch Street to be told that the ladies had come here. I arrived a moment ago and did not wish to interrupt. I saw Darcy the day before Miss Elizabeth left Kent. He could hardly contain his excitement at seeing her again. Perhaps nerves got the best of him, and he rode out to meet her?"

"It is possible," Anne agreed. "He was most impatient in his letters to me on the subject."

"Where would you begin looking?" Mrs. Gardiner asked.

"I suppose at the coaching inns," Richard said. "He would need to rest or change horses often."

"The Bell in Bromley," Elizabeth said. "It is his favourite coaching inn on the route to Rosings. He would certainly stop there. If they have seen him, then search forward, closer to Rosings. If they have not, then work backwards."

"You know his favourite coaching inn?" Richard asked. "I have travelled with him to Rosings these last five years, and I do not think I knew that."

"Why would he not write to me?" Georgiana's bottom lip trembled. "If he were sick or injured, surely he could manage to direct a letter to me."

"Shh, there is no use imagining the worst," Anne said as she gathered Georgiana's hands in hers.

"When can you be off, Bingley?" Richard asked.

"This very minute." He stood. "Or perhaps I should write to my sisters?" He glanced at Jane.

"I will write to Caroline and Louisa for you."

"I need not return to my post for three days," Richard said. He rang the bell for a servant and, when one entered, ordered Darcy's largest carriage to be made ready. "One of us should ride, but I think we should have the coach as we do not know what condition he will be in when we find him."

Georgiana gasped and began to cry. Richard attempted to soothe her, but his eyes met Elizabeth's over his cousin's head. It was far more likely that they might not find him at all or that his situation would be very dire once found.

"Come, girls," Mrs. Gardiner said. "We should allow Mr. Darcy's family privacy as they deal with this matter."

"Please, may Elizabeth stay?" Anne asked with tears in her eyes. "I think Georgie and I could use her good sense and rallying spirit."

Elizabeth silently pleaded with Mrs. Gardiner, and the older lady relented. She and Jane said farewell to the remaining party and departed.

Within half an hour, Richard and Bingley were ready to leave on their mission. The ladies gathered at the main entrance to wish the men well. Unexpectedly, Anne approached Richard and flung her arms around his neck.

"I am tired of hiding, Richard." Then, she leaned on her tiptoes and kissed him.

Richard stumbled backwards in shock for a moment before pulling Anne into his arms. "I am as well." He gave her another quick kiss. "Wish me Godspeed, love. We will discuss this when I return."

Elizabeth met the shocked eyes of Bingley and Georgiana, each wearing grins. Who knew Anne could be so bold? A moment later, the gentlemen left.

Elizabeth suggested that Georgiana perform on the pianoforte, hoping the music would serve as a distraction for the remaining ladies. She knew for herself, however, that her focus would be on that unknown location where Darcy now resided. She fervently prayed he was not injured or deathly ill. The thought of losing him answered Elizabeth's final question regarding Darcy. Whether he returned her love or not, whether he lived or died, her feelings would not vanish. They would endure for her entire life.

Chapter Nine

Darcy frowned as his host handed a muddied letter back to him. "It never reached London?"

"'Fraid not, milord."

"Mrs. Green, how many times do I have to tell you that I am no lord. You may address me as Mr. Darcy, or even Darcy if you please."

"As you say, sir." Despite the elderly woman's twisted hands and hunched back, she busied herself with refilling his glass of water and removing the breakfast dishes. "Surgeon may be 'round today. He can write another fer ya."

Darcy held back his sigh of frustration. She had said the same thing yesterday and the day before. Apparently, the surgeon had more critical calls to make, and the vicar was not in residence this week. If Darcy had not lost his purse when he was thrown from his horse, he might have been able to motivate more help, but as it was, most people were cautious when helping a stranger dressed in fine clothes with not a penny to his person. They must have thought him a titled wastrel. Although he assured them that if someone carried his letter to his London house they would be justly compensated, no one he had met since being found on the side of the road with a broken leg and bleeding head had bothered to try their hand.

Instead of airing his displeasure, Darcy smiled at the lady. "Thank you. I appreciate all that you have done for me."

Mrs. Green's husband and eldest son had found Darcy and loaded him on their cart. He went in and out of consciousness for the first two days. During that time, he heard voices arguing about whether they could afford a surgeon and how best to stop the blood. By the time Mrs. Green went behind her husband's back and called the surgeon, three days had passed, and the setting of his broken leg had been so excruciating he passed out.

Thankfully, the man had waited to see if Darcy would come to before leaving. The first thought on Darcy's mind was that he needed to send a letter to his relations. They would be worried about his absence, and someone must explain to Elizabeth that he was delayed in calling on her.

It was not Mrs. Green's fault or even her husband's that Darcy was in this mess. No, that was all his rotten luck. Bingley's words about admiring his restraint in waiting for Elizabeth to come to London had echoed in his mind all week. He had only one day left to wait and found it impossible. He would ride to Rosings at a breakneck pace, even though it threatened to rain, and remind her of his love in person. They could be assured of more privacy at Rosings than they could in

London. He had hoped she would be more receptive to his courtship. In his wildest dreams, she said enough to prompt another proposal, which was sealed with a kiss.

For once in his life, Darcy had been driven away by passion and acted as insensibly as a man desperately in love might be expected to do. All he now had to show for it was a broken leg, a stitched head, and bruised hands. Elizabeth likely doubted his constancy. Even once he managed to return to London — which might be several weeks from now — the tale was too incredible to believe. He must also be causing Georgiana considerable grief, although he was thankful Richard would be present to lend support. He assumed some search for him would be conducted, but he had said nothing to his servants about his direction. He could hardly form articulate words to call for his horse and pack a bag. Funds would be wasted as they had no idea in which direction to look. First, they would probably assume he had gone to Pemberley and would wait for news from there. After waiting a week, a letter of inquiry would be sent. If they sent one by express, Darcy would still expect a fortnight to pass before anyone began searching for him. Even still, the route to Pemberley would be the most probable route with which to begin.

All the fruitless thinking and self-condemnation fatigued him. Darcy welcomed the blackness of sleep and reprieve from a mess of his own making. He ought to have stayed at Rosings and courted Elizabeth there. Now, he may regret it for the rest of his life.

*****

When he awoke to Richard's and Bingley's voices some time later, Darcy thought he was dreaming.

"Milord is through here," Mrs. Green said. "Don't know if he can be moved. The surgeon needs to see him still."

"Bingley, ride into the town and find the surgeon. Get him here at once. Money is no concern."

Darcy heard quick, heavy steps and managed to open one eye to see Richard staring down at him. "Ah, it is you, Darcy! I thought for sure we had the right place when she called you a lord." Richard laughed before sitting down.

"Damned dream," Darcy said and rubbed his eyes.

"You dream of me? I am flattered, although perhaps we shall not tell Miss Elizabeth that."

Finally convinced that Richard was in the flesh and not a figment of his imagination, Darcy opened his eyes all the way. "Richard! How did you find me?"

"Georgiana thought it odd that you were gone for so long without a word to her. Anne wondered why you did not welcome her in London. Hints were made that you had promised to call at the Gardiner residence the day after Anne and Miss Elizabeth arrived. Before I made it to Darcy House, the lady herself had come, convincing my cousins that you would never break your promise to call on her and that something awful must have befallen you."

Darcy marvelled at Elizabeth's attitude. "Nothing so awful. An animal spooked my horse, and I was sent flying. I broke my leg and cut my head. The difficulty lay in that I lost my purse and could not pay my hosts nor anyone else to ride to London or send an express. I convinced the surgeon, when he finally arrived, to send a note, but it was returned today." He held up the muddied envelope.

Richard peered at it. "It looks as though it was returned several days ago. I am unsurprised. Mail service to these small hamlets is deplorable."

"I do not understand how you thought to look for me in Kent. I had thought you would look on the route to Pemberley first."

"Indeed, I would have," Richard said with a small smile. "I even thought you might have fled to purposefully avoid Miss Elizabeth."

"I would never—"

"I was already reprimanded on the subject. Bingley said he was surprised you did not return to Rosings, and Miss Elizabeth herself was so utterly convinced that you were still madly in love with her. She suggested that we look first at The Bell in Bromley rather than wasting time at every coaching inn. How did she know that was your favourite inn?"

Darcy flushed. "In one of my letters to her, I explained how I loved their Toad in the Hole. I was attempting to make light conversation. I am surprised she remembered."

"Well, it was quite useful and saved us considerable time. Once we determined you had been there, we knew to move forward, and it was not long before we heard a tale of a horse found with no rider. We focused on the neighbouring towns and hamlets and were finally directed here."

Richard leaned close to Darcy's ear. "Why on earth did you not write to us? What are you doing staying in this decrepit building without adequate care?"

Darcy whispered back, "They did the best they could. Beggars cannot be so choosy. I was fortunate that anyone would take care of me at all."

"Well, I can think of three eager ladies who would gladly take care of you once we get you to London."

"Three?"

"Yes, and I think I might have a bone to pick with you. Why did you arrange for Anne to journey to London? Why did you tell me nothing of your plans to court Miss Elizabeth from afar? You should have simply stayed at Rosings."

Fortunately for Darcy, Bingley arrived with the surgeon in tow. Richard's expression said he would not wait long for an explanation. The man poked and prodded before announcing Darcy well enough to travel. He advised it would be quite painful to be moved and suggested an inn rather than several hours in a carriage but understood the necessity. Richard promptly paid the man, and after Darcy explained his gratitude to Mrs. Green and her family, he left her with more money than they likely earned in a year.

After hasty farewells and assistance from Bingley and Richard, Darcy found himself in his carriage with a flask of spirits thrust into his hand to numb the pain. Once sufficiently inebriated, he explained to Richard about his ridiculous plan to woo Elizabeth, how he involved

Anne, and repaid her with her heart's dearest wish — a trip to town without Lady Catherine.

"Of course, I cannot say more about why Anne desired such a journey. I would not want to break her confidence."

At the mention of that, Bingley smirked, and Richard flushed.

"I think Richard knows all about why Miss de Bourgh wished to be in London."

"Really? What happened?"

"She kissed him! In front of your sister, Miss Elizabeth, and me! She ran right up and kissed him. Lucky dog!"

"You have your own lady," Richard growled and playfully knocked into Bingley with his shoulder. "Get your eyes off mine."

"Oh, she is your lady, is she?" Darcy teased.

"No more brandy for you," Richard said and pulled the flask out of Darcy's hand. "You are only jealous because I have what you want."

"A kiss from Anne?" Darcy made a face, making Bingley laugh. "No, thank you."

"No, you idiot." Richard rolled his eyes. "I am surrounded by idiots. I hope we hit a deep rut just to teach you a lesson."

"You would wish that on your favourite cousin?"

"I think I have made plain my preference for my favourite cousin. I surely will not be kissing you, no matter how much you dream of me."

"Darcy dreams of you?" Bingley asked, a horrified expression on his face.

"Lord, no!" Darcy glared at his cousin. "When he first entered the room back there, I thought I was dreaming and mumbled something to the effect."

"And you will not put me off teasing you that you want a kiss from Miss Elizabeth."

"Now, don't be sore, Richard. It's only because she's prettier than you." Darcy laughed and then promptly fell asleep.

Five hours later, Richard shook Darcy awake. "We are here. It is time to get you into bed."

"I need to see Elizabeth," Darcy said, ignoring the throbbing in his head and leg. "Let us go to Gracechurch Street."

"Darcy, it's far too late to call on the Gardiners. Besides, when we left, Elizabeth was invited to stay at Darcy House. She is likely still awake and waiting for news about you."

"No one sent an express?"

Richard and Bingley looked at each other and shook their heads. Some pair of rescuers they were.

"I hope she can forgive me," Darcy muttered.

"Forgive you! You had an accident," Richard said from one side. "A completely avoidable accident all because of your foolishness but an accident nevertheless."

"If I were a lady, I think I would like the reckless display of impulse." Bingley slid an arm around Darcy's other shoulder.

"You would," Darcy and Richard answered in unison before laughing.

That was how they entered Darcy House. The two friends providing support for the man in the middle with smiles on their faces and laughter on their lips. As soon as the door shut, there was a scurry of footsteps in an unladylike pace. A thud hit Darcy and almost knocked him over.

"Careful, Elizabeth!" Anne chided. "He is hurt."

Richard and Bingley let go of Darcy, and he leaned against the warmth of his beloved.

"Welcome home, Fitzwilliam," Georgiana said from somewhere. Darcy only had eyes for Elizabeth, though, so he could not be sure where his sister stood. "I am pleased you are in one piece!"

"Georgie," Richard said, "call the housekeeper. We will need chambers made ready, bandages, and tonics. I think an apothecary or surgeon can wait until morning. How about I tell you how I rescued Darcy by myself—"

"I helped!" Bingley cried.

"Your lady is not here now. We can change the story tomorrow."

Anne laughed. "Is that what soldiers do? Change their stories to impress ladies?"

"The first rule of warfare is to impress your lady — just one."

"We cannot leave Fitzwilliam and Elizabeth here," Georgiana said.

There was silence and Darcy was sure that the others looked at him and Elizabeth in each other's arms, but he did not care. He had promised Elizabeth when she made it to London that no one would be left in doubt of his love, least of all her, and he would not let go of her until she moved first.

Richard finally spoke. "I think they can make it to his study. They need a few minutes to speak to one another."

Darcy heard their footsteps fade down the hall and up the stairs. Elizabeth finally looked up from where her face was buried in Darcy's coat. Tears shimmered in her eyes. "Lean on me. We can go slow."

Fortunately, the study was only a few feet from the entrance. Between Elizabeth's assistance and gripping the wall and various objects, Darcy made it safely to a chair. He sagged in relief. Elizabeth began to move away, but Darcy pulled her to balance on his good leg.

"Fitzwilliam!" she cried in surprise.

Darcy grinned. "Yes, Elizabeth?"

"This is hardly proper."

"Neither is our being alone, you embracing me, you arriving at my townhouse to insist that I must be madly in love with you—"

"Or you writing to me and having your cousin do your work?"

Darcy chuckled. "It seems we never understood one another when we abided by the rules of propriety. You can hardly blame me for not wanting to give up the feel of you in my arms. I have waited so long for it."

Elizabeth nodded and rested her head on his shoulder. "I feared I lost you," she whispered. "I thought I was blinded by prejudice for too long and lost my chance with you. I almost gave you up."

"I am sorry for that. In a moment of impulse, I decided to ride to Rosings and declare my love once more. I ought not to have been so reckless."

Elizabeth's breath caught. "You were so impassioned as that? I knew it would be a sight to behold."

"Why did you not give up on me, my love?" Darcy caressed Elizabeth's cheek and felt it warm with his question.

"I had come to see your steadfast character whilst at Rosings. Even more than believing you would not abandon me without a word, my heart insisted you still loved me."

"Why did it do that?" He already knew, but he had been desperate for many weeks to hear the words from her.

Elizabeth lifted her face from his shoulder and met his eyes. She placed one of Darcy's hands over her heart and held it there. "I knew you still loved me because I love you. Our hearts are one."

Darcy was unsure who moved first, but soon he found their lips touching in the sweetest bliss he had ever known. After pulling back and taking in the dazed expression on Elizabeth's face, he kissed her nose. "Will you marry me?"

"Yes!" Elizabeth cocked her head to one side. "I should have accepted the first time, but then I would not have had your courtship at Rosings."

They shared a laugh before their lips met again. They were interrupted too soon but knew they would have a lifetime ahead to share embraces and kisses. In the weeks that followed, Darcy healed, and their wedding was planned.

In early June, a triple wedding was held for Darcy, Richard, and Bingley and their beautiful brides. Although Lady Catherine was at first indignant that Darcy had not chosen her daughter, her complaints ceased when Lord Fitzwilliam gifted his younger son with a small estate, and there was talk of giving him a title due to his experience in the war. Appalled at the lack of discretion in the youngest Bennet daughters, she invited them to Rosings where they were separated from the evil effects of the militia. Through the connections of their brothers-in-law, they married well. At Easter each year, the extended family met at Rosings, where Darcy and Elizabeth could reminisce about their secret courtship.

The End

Before you go

Thank you so much for reading Courtship at Rosings! If you enjoyed this book, please consider leaving a review at the retailer of your choice.

Mr. Darcy's Compassion

A sample from Mr. Darcy's Compassion

Chapter One

Darcy peered out his carriage window as the conveyance rolled to a halt before the coaching inn at his usual stop in South Mimms. To the east about twenty miles lay the town of Meryton, Hertfordshire. As often as he had traversed the roads between London and Pemberley, he had never before considered what lay beyond them. His mind had only considered the path before him and the duties attached to the destination. Whether at his estate or his London home, his responsibilities to family and legacy did not cease. Despite knowing Meryton lay only a few hours away, and with it the woman he loved, he would cling to his usual route.

Inside the tavern portion of the inn, Darcy grimaced when told that the private dining areas were full and his usual suites unavailable. His decision to leave London for Pemberley was formed suddenly, only hours ago. Easter with his sister in their ancestral home was a convenient excuse. Georgiana's companion indicated that she was recovered enough to see him. Traditionally, Darcy visited his maternal aunt for the holiday. However, he was now sickened by high society and anyone who kept their views. Waving off the proprietor's concern for his offence, Darcy sat in the loud common room.

He glanced around the area, unsurprised to see he had no acquaintances in the crowded chamber. A movement out of the corner of his eye caught his notice. The maid moved with too much grace; her gown seemed too fine to be the usual sort. Was she some fancy piece trying to sell her wares? It was unlike Cuthbert to allow such, but who was Darcy to interfere with a man's business? As the lady's movements and figure continued to interest him—and invariably remind him of a lady mere miles away—he cursed under his breath for the fact that he now compared every woman born high or low to Elizabeth Bennet.

What would his family and friends say if they knew of his obsession? The earl would glare. Lady Catherine would lecture and throw her daughter at him. Bingley would laugh, and Richard, his cousin, would suggest he enjoy the barmaid's enticements and be free of his physical longing—and possibly mental torment as well. Darcy had too much honour for such, however, and so when he waved her over it was only with the intent to order refreshment. Never mind the fact that her laugh at the table next to him reminded him too much of Elizabeth's, and he had relished the warm sound when it washed over him.

"What would you like?" she asked.

Her voice was very like Elizabeth's. Darcy kicked himself again for allowing her to make such a slave of him that his imagination could go so far as to hear her voice. Looking up from his hands, their eyes met, and Darcy's breath caught.

Elizabeth gasped. "Mr. Darcy!"

"Eliza—Miss Bennet!"

"Par—pardon me!" Elizabeth laid her tray of ale down in a clatter and ran from the room.

Darcy stared after her. Why on earth was she serving in a tavern twenty miles from her home? The Bennets had not been as wealthy as he or Bingley, but their estate was prosperous enough. Only financial hardship or extreme love could drive her to such a situation. Darcy knew the owner of the inn and knew the Bennets had no relationship to him, which left only the financial motive. Before he could think better of it, he was in front of Cuthbert and tossing several pounds at him.

"That maid—the one who just ran out of the room—"

"Lizzy? Pretty with big, brown eyes?"

Darcy nodded. "Yes, that's the one. I'm paying her wages for the week. Find another maid."

Several men around him broke into laughter and raised an obscene toast in his honour, but he cared not one whit. As he dodged puddles of ale and urine, he followed through the door where Elizabeth exited. Hearing sobbing down the hall, he turned and then crept up the stairs. His heart beat in his throat with every step. There was another reason she could be here, one which lay heavily on his mind. Wickham might have ruined her. Darcy ought to have openly declared to the world that man's character. He should have told Elizabeth the truth and warned her. Instead, his pride demanded he keep his failings private. If Wickham had not ruined Elizabeth, she might have been raped by any man down below. He did not think she would willingly sell herself, but many men took no heed of a negative answer.

Elizabeth sat on the top of the stairs, her head buried in her hands. The sounds of despair and agony split through him. Darcy bent at the knee and placed a hand on her shoulder, intent on offering her a handkerchief and escorting her to the safety of a room.

Before he could speak, he was struck on the side of his head. The unexpected movement set him tumbling down several stairs, landing hard on one arm. Along the way, he reached for the railing managing to twist his arm in a painful contortion.

"How dare you!" Elizabeth cried out, followed a moment later by, "Oh good Lord! What have I done? Mr. Darcy?"

"Aye," Darcy moaned.

"I am so sorry," she stammered. "I thought you were a stranger set on accosting me..."

The pain in Darcy's heart upon hearing such words could be surpassed only by the pain he felt in his arm. He heard Elizabeth's quick steps and a snivel as she wiped her tears away.

"Can you move?" she asked gently once at his side.

"I think so." He made to roll over, and she assisted him. No longer lying on his injured arm, it throbbed even worse as blood rushed around it.

"We should get you to your room and call the surgeon." Elizabeth held her hand out to assist him with his uninjured arm.

As his hand gripped around hers, he noted the rough nature of her palm and digits. Mere weeks ago, they would have been as soft as any gentlewoman's. What kind of life had she endured since he left Hertfordshire?

"We can get to the guest chambers through here." Elizabeth opened a door near the second-floor landing where he had fallen. "Your room must be this way."

"I am on the third floor, actually." Darcy winced as each step sent a jolt to his arm.

"Very well," Elizabeth said in a confused voice.

That she seemed unfamiliar with the layout brought him some comfort. "Here, room six, I believe they said."

He knocked, and his valet opened the door. "Mr. Darcy." Stevens glanced from Darcy to Elizabeth rapidly before he, at last, seemed to realise that Darcy oddly held his arm. "Is all well?'

"It is not," Darcy said as the servant stepped aside so he could enter. "I have badly sprained my arm. Please, see if a surgeon is available."

"Of course, sir. The lady's bag arrived a moment ago."

Noting that Stevens dashed away rather than be present for the necessary discussion, Darcy shuffled to the table and chair in the room. He could be treated there, and staying away from his bed would likely help Elizabeth's sensibilities.

"I am so sorry, Mr. Darcy," Elizabeth said, blushing. "I will leave you and your...guest." She glanced around, and her eyes fell on her bag. Immediately, she stiffened. "Just why are my things in your chamber?"

"Cuthbert must have needed the room. I suppose he has already found your replacement."

"My replacement!"

"Well, I paid him for your wages."

"You bought me?"

Darcy could hear in Elizabeth's tone her anger and surprise, emotions he thought would soon fade. However, he had not expected the look of utter anguish to haunt her eyes. "No, I paid the man for the trouble of hiring a new maid and secured you safe lodgings until I can deliver you to Longbourn."

"I will never go back there. Never."

Download now!

Acknowledgments

To my author friends Leenie and Zoe that always were willing to hold my hand, nothing can take your place in my heart.

Special thanks to my editor, Anna Horner.

Thank you to the countless other people of the JAFF community who have inspired and encouraged me.

Last, but not least, I could never have written, let alone published, without the love and support of my beloved husband and babies!

About the Author

Born in the wrong era, Rose Fairbanks has read nineteenth-century novels since childhood. Although she studied history, her transcript also contains every course in which she could discuss Jane Austen. Never having given up all-nighters for reading, Rose discovered her love for Historical Romance after reading Christi Caldwell's Heart of a Duke Series.

After a financial downturn and her husband's unemployment had threatened her ability to stay at home with their special needs child, Rose began writing the kinds of stories she had loved to read for so many years. Now, a best-selling author of Jane Austen-inspired stories, she also writes Regency Romance, Historical Fiction, Paranormal Romance, and Historical Fantasy.

Having completed a BA in history in 2008, she plans to finish her master's studies someday. When not reading or writing, Rose runs after her two young children, ignores housework, and profusely thanks her husband for doing all the dishes and laundry. She is a member of the Jane Austen Society of North America and Romance Writers of America.

You can connect with Rose on Facebook,Instagram, Pinterest, and her blog: http://rosefairbanks.com

To join her email list for information about new releases and any other news, you can sign up here: http://eepurl.com/bmJHjn

Facebook fans! Join Rose's reading groups:

Rose's Reading Garden

Jane Austen Re-Imaginings Series

Christmas with Jane

When Love Blooms Series

Pride and Prejudice and Bluestockings Series

Loving Elizabeth Series

More from Rose Fairbanks

Jane Austen Re-Imaginings Series

(STAND ALONE SERIES)

Letters from the Heart
Undone Business
No Cause to Repine
Love Lasts Longest
Mr. Darcy's Kindness
Mr. Darcy's Compassion

When Love Blooms Series

Sufficient Encouragement
Renewed Hope
Extraordinary Devotion

Loving Elizabeth Series

Pledged
Reunited

Treasured
Loving Elizabeth Collection (Books 1-3)

Pride and Prejudice and Bluestockings

Mr. Darcy's Bluestocking Bride
Lady Darcy's Bluestocking Club (Coming 2020)

Impertinent Daughters Series

The Gentleman's Impertinent Daughter
Mr. Darcy's Impertinent Daughter (Coming 2020)

Desire and Obligation Series

A Sense of Obligation
Domestic Felicity (Coming 2020)

Christmas with Jane

Once Upon a December
Mr. Darcy's Miracle at Longbourn
How Darcy Saved Christmas

Men of Austen

The Secrets of Pemberley
The Secrets of Donwell Abbey (*Emma* Variation,
Coming 2020)

Regency Romance

Flowers of Scotland (Marriage Maker Series)

The Maid of Inverness

Paranormal Regency Fairy Tale

Cinderella's Phantom Prince and Beauty's Mirror (with Jenni James)

Printed in Great Britain
by Amazon

57792750R00068